PUFFIN CANADA

FOOL'S GOLD

ERIC WALTERS, a former elementary school
teacher, has written over forty acclaimed and
bestselling novels, including *War of the
Eagles*, *Trapped in Ice*, *S.T.A.R.S.*, *Rebound*
and *Run*. He lives in Mississauga, Ontario.

CAMP X
FOOL'S GOLD

ERIC WALTERS

PUFFIN
CANADA

PUFFIN CANADA

Published by the Penguin Group

Penguin Group (Canada), 90 Eglinton Avenue East, Suite 700, Toronto, Ontario, Canada
M4P 2Y3 (a division of Pearson Canada Inc.)

Penguin Group (USA) Inc., 375 Hudson Street, New York, New York 10014, U.S.A.
Penguin Books Ltd, 80 Strand, London WC2R 0RL, England
Penguin Ireland, 25 St Stephen's Green, Dublin 2, Ireland (a division of Penguin Books Ltd)
Penguin Group (Australia), 250 Camberwell Road, Camberwell, Victoria 3124, Australia
(a division of Pearson Australia Group Pty Ltd)
Penguin Books India Pvt Ltd, 11 Community Centre, Panchsheel Park, New Delhi – 110 017,
India
Penguin Group (NZ), 67 Apollo Drive, Rosedale, North Shore 0632, Auckland, New Zealand
(a division of Pearson New Zealand Ltd)
Penguin Books (South Africa) (Pty) Ltd, 24 Sturdee Avenue, Rosebank, Johannesburg 2196,
South Africa

Penguin Books Ltd, Registered Offices: 80 Strand, London WC2R 0RL, England

First published in a Puffin Canada hardcover by Penguin Group (Canada),
a division of Pearson Canada Inc., 2006
Published in this edition, 2007

1 2 3 4 5 6 7 8 9 10 (OPM)

LIBRARY AND ARCHIVES CANADA CATALOGUING IN PUBLICATION

Walters, Eric, 1957–
Fool's gold : Camp X / Eric Walters.

ISBN 978-0-670-06542-4 (bound).—ISBN 978-0-14-331255-0 (pbk.)

I. Title.

PS8595.A598F66 2006   jC813'.54   C2006-902302-6

ISBN-13: 978-0-14-331255-0
ISBN-10: 0-14-331255-3

Visit the Penguin Group (Canada) website at **www.penguin.ca**

Special and corporate bulk purchase rates available; please see
www.penguin.ca/corporatesales or call 1-800-810-3104, ext. 477 or 474

CHAPTER ONE

I TOSSED THE NEWSPAPER and it skimmed over the railing and onto the porch, landing just off to the right side of the front door of the house.

"That makes three perfect pitches in a row!" I shouted.

"Impressive … that is, if you'd said *ten* instead of three!" Jack yelled back across the street. He heaved another paper and I watched as it soared onto the porch, skidding to a stop right in front of the door—a perfect strike.

"Make that, I'd be impressed if it was *eleven* in a row!" Jack called out.

Eleven in a row for me wouldn't just be impressive, it would be impossible. I didn't have my big brother's arm—yet—or his amazing ability to be a pain.

This was our second paper route. When we'd lived in Whitby for a while we'd delivered papers there. Then we moved here to Bowmanville. I was hoping this was going to be our last stop in working our way across the province delivering papers.

We continued to move down the street, Jack on one side, me on the other. Our route had nearly two hundred houses and already I knew every one. Maybe I didn't have my brother's arm, but I was definitely his match when it came to memory.

My brother finished the last house on his side of the street—perfect toss number twelve, I was sure—and he crossed over and joined me.

"Which job do you like better," I asked, "paper route or delivering the mail to Camp 30?"

He thought for a moment as we walked, then said, "Delivering the mail. I miss the camp."

Camp 30 was the prisoner-of-war camp just outside of town. Some of the most important, highest-ranking German prisoners were locked up there, sent to Canada after being captured in the war. That's where our mother worked, as an assistant to the commander, Colonel Armstrong. Our father was fighting in Africa, with the St. Patrick's Regiment, and it felt like he'd been gone forever.

During the summer we'd been hired by Colonel Armstrong to pick up the prisoners' mail from the post office in town and bring it up to the camp. That was our *official* job. Our unofficial job—something that nobody at the camp, not Colonel Armstrong, not even our own *mother* knew about—was to secretly gather information about the prisoners. After all, who would suspect a twelve-year-old and his fourteen-year-old brother of being spies?

I guess that should have been a pretty safe job—delivering the mail and keeping our eyes and ears open, passing on anything important that we picked up—but somehow the words "Jack" and "safe" don't usually go in the same sentence.

It turned out the prisoners were planning an escape through a tunnel they'd been digging. Because of Jack's pushing and prodding we discovered the tunnel—and the prisoners discovered us. They grabbed us and took us along on the escape. They hauled us all the way to the St. Lawrence River, near Cornwall, where a submarine was coming to pick them up and take them back to Germany. We'd probably have been eating sauerkraut and schnitzel today if the good guys hadn't shown up just in time to blow that submarine out of the water.

What a story—and we hadn't told a soul. The only people who knew what had happened to us were the guys who'd asked us to be spies in the first place, the guys we'd first met at Camp X, when we'd lived in Whitby. Camp X was a training camp for spies, and Jack and I had discovered it almost by accident. That's where we'd met Bill, our contact at the camp, and his boss, Little Bill. Little Bill was the top boss, sort of the head spy of everybody. And, of course, nobody knew about what happened to us there, either—Nazi spies trying to break into the camp, us almost getting our heads blown off, stealing a jeep and … again, it seemed hard to believe that any of it was true, or that it had actually happened to me and Jack.

"I still don't know why they wouldn't let us continue to deliver the mail after the escape attempt," Jack said.

"I guess they just wanted us to do something safer."

"And you think delivering papers is safe?" Jack asked. "We could get hit by a truck or attacked by a big, mean dog."

"Or get a paper cut," I added.

Jack smiled. "Maybe it's best this way, anyway," he said.

"It is?" That didn't sound like Jack.

"Yeah. We've been dodging bullets."

"A couple, I guess."

"I don't mean like real bullets … although there have been a few of those … I mean like bad things happening. So far we've managed to avoid everything."

"Well, not everything. I got two concussions and you had a broken arm and a broken jaw and—"

"But we didn't get *killed*. We've been lucky so far, and we can't count on being lucky forever."

"I guess you're right."

"It's good to get out while we're still alive and in one piece," Jack said.

"Yeah, that makes sense. But do you think we're *really* out of it … is it all over?" I asked.

Jack tossed another paper and it hit the railing and bounced back, landing on the grass. I stifled the urge to laugh. As he walked over to retrieve the paper I grabbed one out of my bag and tossed it—it sailed over the railing, hit the bottom of the door with a loud thud and landed on the doormat.

"That makes four!" I exclaimed.

Jack picked up his off-target paper. I half expected him to throw it at me but instead he stuffed it back in his bag.

"To answer your question, I do think that it's probably all over," he said. "I think that we stumbled into the first adventure and then bumbled into the second. There's not going to be a third."

That made sense. But I wasn't sure if I should feel relieved or disappointed.

"Do you think we'll ever see any of them again?" I asked.

"Bill and Little Bill?" Jack asked.

I nodded.

"Maybe Bill. He turns up at the strangest times and places. But I think Little Bill is probably too busy."

"I guess you're right. Besides, Bill is just down the road at Camp X, and Little Bill could be anywhere. Didn't Bill once say that Little Bill worked from New York and London?"

"I think I remember that. Let's just hurry and finish delivering the papers." Jack looked at his watch. "Supper is going to be ready soon."

That was all the incentive I needed. I was hungry. And we only had three more streets to go.

"I'll take Maple, you can do Elm, and I'll meet you on Staples," I suggested.

"Works for me. Make sure you don't miss any houses," Jack warned.

"It's guaranteed that I'm *going* to miss houses," I said.

Jack skidded to a stop.

"I'm going to miss the houses that aren't supposed to get papers." I laughed and hurried off, leaving Jack standing there looking annoyed. Hey, he wasn't the *only* one who could be annoying!

We moved along Staples Street as quickly as possible. We were half walking, half running. I was quickly working up a sweat. It was almost five o'clock but it was still really hot—a lot hotter than you'd expect for the middle of September. I wanted to slow down and catch my breath but there was no way I could do that without getting a tongue-lashing from Jack. This was the last street on our route. The way we had the route planned, we finished with the papers on the street just over from ours. Jack showed no sign of slowing down. He probably wouldn't stop until we got home.

"I've been thinking about Superman!" I shouted across the street.

"What?"

"Superman. I was thinking about how it would be if he fought for the Allies. He could end the war in two minutes flat."

Jack stopped and glared at me. "What are you talking about?"

"What don't you understand? You know Superman, right?"

"Of course I know Superman."

"If he fought against the Nazis he could end the war really fast."

"You're wrong," Jack said.

"I don't know how you can even argue! If Superman fought against the Nazis we'd win in a minute!"

"Nope, you're wrong."

"How can I be wrong? He has X-ray vision, superhuman strength, and he can fly! He'd just fly in, grab Hitler and rip that little moustache right off his face and—"

"Kryptonite bullets."

"What?" I questioned.

"Bullets made of kryptonite," he said. "They'd make them and then shoot them when Superman showed his face and … this is stupid! We're arguing about a stupid comic book character! Kryptonite isn't real, Superman isn't real! I don't know why I'm wasting my time even talking about this, and if you bring it up again you're going to need Superman to protect you!"

I shut up. My plan to slow Jack down had worked. I struggled to suppress a smile. I had to fight the urge to start talking now about what it would be like if *Batman* were fighting for the Allies.

"I'm thirsty," Jack said.

"Me too." I was hot and sweaty and hungry, as well. "I hope supper's on the table when we get home."

"Going to find out pretty soon."

We bounded up the walk, up the steps, onto the porch and through the front door.

"Something's wrong," Jack said.

"What?"

"Smell," he said.

"Smell what? I don't smell any …" I didn't smell pot roast. I didn't smell anything.

"Maybe Mom got supper started late," I suggested.

"Mom!" Jack yelled. There was no answer. I followed Jack as he walked toward the kitchen, pushed through the door and—Mom was sitting in a chair at the kitchen table. Beside her stood three men, guns in hand. One gun was pointed at our mother's head, and the other two guns were aimed directly at me and Jack!

CHAPTER TWO

I BUMPED INTO JACK as he skidded to a stop. My *heart* skidded to a stop. We stood there, frozen in place, unable to react to what I couldn't believe I was seeing, too stunned to even feel afraid. I looked at Mom. I could tell she was trying to look brave and calm, but I could see she was biting the inside of her lip—a nervous habit that we shared.

"Welcome," one of the men said. "Sit." He motioned with his gun to the two empty chairs beside our mother.

Neither of us moved. For a split second I thought about running, breaking for the door and—

"Now!" he ordered, and Jack and I stumbled forward. We slumped into the chairs.

"That's better." He took his gun and put it into a holster under his suit jacket. The other two did the same. They were all dressed in fancy dark suits and ties. They wore felt fedora hats and shiny leather dress shoes. They looked like they were dressed to go to a wedding … or a funeral. I swallowed hard.

"You must be wondering who we are," the same man said.

"We know who you are," Jack snarled.

"Do you?" he asked.

"You're a bunch of stinking Nazi agents!"

Two of the men burst into laughter until the third—I guessed he was the leader—held up his hand.

"We're not Nazis ... although I can understand why you'd think that."

Now that he'd told us who they *weren't* I was waiting for him to tell us who they *were*.

"Please leave us alone. I've told you that you have the wrong people!" our mother exclaimed.

She sounded desperate, and I noticed that there were streaks on her cheeks—dried-up tracks of tears. If they'd hurt her in any way I'd—

"And I told *you* that we had the *right* people. Jack and George Braun. That is who the two of you are, isn't it?"

I wanted to tell them that we weren't but I knew that wouldn't work.

"Yes, they're my sons, Jack and George. But they're just two boys ... they can't possibly have anything that you want!" she pleaded.

"That's where you're wrong. They have something that I definitely need." He paused. "They have information ... about Camp X."

"No, no, there's definitely been a mistake! I've never even heard of a Camp X. I work at Camp *30,* and they used to deliver mail there during the summer, but honestly they know practically nothing about it!"

The man smiled. "I know where you work. I also know that the boys are very, *very* familiar with Camp X."

Who were these men, and how did they know about us and Camp X? Maybe they didn't. Maybe they were trying to trick us into believing they knew more than they actually did. I tried to keep my face completely blank, to not reveal anything. I even stopped myself from chewing on the inside of my cheek—I didn't want them to know I was nervous. But then again, why shouldn't I be nervous? No, not nervous, *terrified*. The initial shock, the numbness, had worn off now and in its place I felt a gut-wrenching fear.

"Do one of you boys want to tell your mother about your involvement with Camp X?" the man asked.

"We have nothing to tell," Jack said. His fists were balled up and he was staring at the man with angry, intense eyes. He looked so brave, so strong. "We don't know what you're talking about."

"Please, there's no need to lie," the man said. His words were suddenly gentle, his tone friendly. There was a smile on his face. If it wasn't for the fancy suit—and the *gun* tucked *inside* that fancy suit—he could have been a teacher, or even a minister.

"Your sons are very brave," he said to our mother. "And loyal. They don't want to say they know anything about Camp X because that would violate the oaths they signed under the Official Secrets Act."

"They're just boys … they didn't sign anything, they don't even know about things like that," our mother said.

"It isn't nice for boys to keep secrets from their mother, but they signed those oaths before you moved to Bowmanville." He paused. "Did you ever wonder how you got your new job at Camp 30?"

"Who are you?" I blurted out. I didn't want anybody to talk about that. She couldn't find out.

"Good to see you haven't swallowed your tongue. You must be wondering how we know so much. As I said, we are not Nazi agents. We have no time or tolerance for the Nazis."

If they weren't Nazis, who could they be? I was struck by the strangest thought. Maybe these guys were working for Bill, and this was a test to see if we'd break our oath, and … No, it couldn't be that. He wouldn't spill the beans to our mother, or scare her like this.

"We are businessmen," he said.

"You mean mobsters?" Jack asked.

"Mobsters?" he asked. "Do we look like mobsters?"

I studied the three men. They were all dressed the same—and they *did* look like they'd just walked out of a mobster movie. The one doing all the talking was older, maybe in his forties, and I was sure he was the boss. One of the other two had a baby face on top of a gigantic body. He towered over everybody else, and his arms and chest were massive. He didn't look like he needed a gun to threaten somebody. The third was short—a couple of inches shorter than Jack—but he was stocky and powerful through the arms and shoulders. He looked as though he could take care of himself as well.

"If you're not Nazis and you're not mobsters, then who are you?" Jack asked.

"As I said, we are independent businessmen," he answered.

"And what do you want with us?" Jack demanded.

"There is something at Camp X, something very valuable, that we'd like to get our hands on. We need some information and some help from you boys. Now, who's going to telling us what we need to know?" he asked.

"Don't expect us to cooperate with anything," Jack said.

The leader nodded his head and turned to the little guy. "I told you they wouldn't scare easily."

"Just give me a minute with them and I guarantee they'll be scared," he said.

Now I was really frightened. There was something about the slight smile on his face. I just knew he wouldn't hesitate to hurt us, and that maybe he'd even enjoy it. I also knew that no matter what he did, he wasn't getting me to say anything.

"No," the leader said. "Not yet." He turned back to face us. "We believe in loyalty too. We would never squeal or betray a member of our organization. But sometimes your choices become limited. Tell you what, I'll save you boys the trouble of breaking your oath. I'll do the talking."

"Don't believe anything he says!" I exclaimed to our mother. "None of it is true."

"I certainly hope it *is* true," he said. "Because if it isn't we will have no choice but to kill the three of you."

His words sent a chill up my spine and I felt myself start to shake. It wasn't just the words, it was the way he'd said them. His voice was quiet, gentle, friendly and so matter-of-fact, like he was talking about inviting us out for dinner.

"Your boys were involved at Camp X," he began.

"I don't even know what this Camp X *is*," our mother said.

"It is a training camp for Allied spies, the biggest spy base in all of North America. It's located in Whitby, close to where you once lived."

"I don't know anything about it, but even if it was there, what could my boys have to do with it?" she asked.

"A lot. At first they just stumbled into the camp, breaching security accidentally. Then they were enlisted by one of the men in charge—his name is

Bill—to try to break into the camp, as well as break into the DIL plant." He paused. "Did you know the boys once came out to visit you at work, pretending that you had forgotten your lunch, but they were actually smuggling in a fake bomb to test the security of the munitions factory?"

My mother looked stunned. I felt stunned. How did this man know these things?

"No," he said, shaking his head. "You never knew anything about that. Just like you don't know how your boys were really injured when they landed in the hospital, or how Mr. Krum, the newspaper editor, was really killed. You know nothing." He shook his head slowly and then turned to face Jack and me. "You must be surprised that I know all of these things, aren't you?"

Neither of us answered, but he was right.

"Is there anything you boys would like to say?" he asked.

There were a lot of things I wanted to say. Instead I kept my mouth shut, my face blank, and I stopped myself, again, from chewing on the inside of my cheek.

"Now I'm going to tell you something that none of you know. I'm going to tell you what we want from Camp X and, more importantly, how you two boys are going to help us get it. It is very simple. We want gold."

"Gold?" I said. "They don't have any gold."

The man laughed, and instantly I realized what I'd done. I'd let on that I *did* know something about Camp X.

"And how would you know that?" my mother asked.

"He knows a lot, but he doesn't know about the gold," the man said, before I could think of what to say, or *not* say, in answer to her question.

"The gold is being stored in the catacombs, a series of caves," he went on.

I knew about the caves. I'd seen them before, close to the cliffs above Lake Ontario. But why would he think that there was any gold there?

"This gold is the property of the Bank of England … in fact, it's the entire reserves of the Bank of England."

"But … but why would that be here in Canada instead of in England?" our mother asked.

"Precaution. It was all moved here when there were fears that England would be invaded. It was brought here to keep it out of Hitler's filthy hands."

"But what has any of that got to do with us?" Jack asked.

"You're going to get us into the camp."

"Us?"

"We know that you've snuck in there a couple of times, and now you're going to get *us* in," he said.

"But even if we could—and I'm not saying we know anything about it—how do you think you could get away with all of that gold?"

"We don't want all of the gold. Just some of it. As much as two men," he said, gesturing to his partners, "and two boys can carry."

"Look," Jack said, "even if we did get in once, what makes you think that we can do it again?"

"We can all only hope that you can. If not, then the results could be fatal."

He put a hand on our mother's shoulder, and Jack jumped to his feet. "You leave her alone or I'll—"

The big guy reached out, grabbed Jack and slammed him back into his seat.

"Don't try to be no hero," the man said. "We don't want to hurt nobody. All we want is the gold. So are you gonna cooperate?"

I looked at Jack. He didn't even look in my direction.

"I'm not afraid to die," Jack said.

A small gasp escaped from our mother.

"Really? Me, I'd rather live," the man replied. He walked over and stood right above me. "And you, George, would you choose death over dishonour?"

"I'm not helping you."

"Very noble. Maybe we're just wasting our time. We'll leave now."

"What?" I asked, not believing my ears.

"Leave. If you refuse to cooperate, we'll just leave. Of course, we'll have to kill all three of you first."

My eyes widened in shock.

"We have no choice. No witnesses."

Jack snorted. "If we helped you, even if we helped you get the gold, what would stop you from just killing us all anyway?"

"Very important question. We won't harm you because you're going to become our business partners. We're going to cut you boys in on the profits. We're going to give you one of the bars of gold. Then, if you do tell somebody, you'll end up in jail too. Betray us and you get arrested. Keep your mouth shut and wind up rich."

"We don't want anything that doesn't belong to us," I said.

"But you will take it. That way we'll buy your silence. If you betray us, we won't be the only ones to suffer. You'll be arrested. You'll be seen as traitors. Do you know what they do with traitors?"

"They shoot them," I said under my breath.

That slight smile returned to his face and he nodded. "You now have three days to think through a plan and put it into effect."

"You're going to hold us for three days?" Jack asked.

"Not all of you. Just your mother."

"Our mother?"

"Yes, she'll be coming with us."

"You're not taking our mother anywhere!" Jack yelled and jumped to his feet.

Like lightning the two thugs jumped forward, grabbed Jack and slammed him back into his seat again.

The man—the leader—didn't react to either what Jack had done or the way his men had handled it. Instead he pulled a slip of paper out of his pocket and put it down on the table.

"Here is a phone number. When you've thought through your plan, you call and my men will come back. In the meantime, and until you return with the gold, your mother will be our guest. It's time to go."

The man helped our mother to her feet. Her knees buckled and his hold on her arm steadied her.

"What he's saying," our mother said, "about the camp, about you knowing about it … is it true?"

Jack shook his head. "We can't tell you."

"I think you just did. I can't believe I didn't know anything about it … that you kept it all from me."

"We didn't have a choice," Jack said. "Honestly. We were just trying to protect you."

Jack slowly rose to his feet. I was surprised that neither of the men at his side stopped him this time. He walked over until he stood right in front of the man.

"If you harm her in any way—in *any way*—I'll kill you." He said the words quietly, with no anger.

The man didn't react other than to nod his head. "Jack, if any other fourteen-year-old said that I would see it as an idle, meaningless threat."

"It's more than a threat," Jack said, "it's a promise."

"I believe you," the man said. "And you should believe me. If you do as you're told, then your mother will be returned to you and everybody will become wealthy. If you do your job, your mother will not have a hair on her head harmed. Do we have a deal?" He reached out his hand to Jack like he wanted to shake.

I half expected Jack to spit in his eye or— Jack and the man shook hands!

"Wise. Now for a few details. It is important that nobody gets suspicious about your family's sudden disappearance. One of you has to call your mother's work and then your school to explain that the family is ill. Say it's the measles so nobody will come to the house."

"We'll make the calls," Jack said.

"I'm counting on you, Jack … and so is your mother."

"Remember what I told you," Jack said.

"I will. And one more thing you should remember. I'm sure you're not thinking about going to the police, but in case you're planning on trying to get help from your friends at Camp X, you have to know that we'll know."

"You have somebody inside the camp?" I asked.

He smiled. "How do you think we know so much about the place, about the two of you? If you try to contact Bill—who you know you can trust—that doesn't mean that the message won't be intercepted, or that somebody else won't be aware of your conversation. Are you willing to take that risk with your mother's life? Now, we have to leave."

"Can I just say goodbye to my sons … give them a hug?" my mother asked.

Nobody objected, and the man released her. She walked over and wrapped an arm around each of us and pulled us close. She pressed her face between us.

"Call the police," she whispered. "Don't worry about what will happen to me."

I wanted to tell her we wouldn't do that, but I couldn't. I could only answer with silence.

"It's time," the man said.

Our mother released her grip, but she kept looking into our eyes, as though pleading with us to save ourselves and not worry about her.

"I love you boys."

"We love you too," I stammered, and Jack nodded.

The two men led her out of the kitchen. The third—the leader—stood in the doorway to stop us from following.

"Remember, you only have three days …"

He didn't need to finish the sentence for me to know what would happen if we took longer.

He turned and left, and Jack and I bumped into each other as we stumbled after him. We heard the door slam and got to the front window in time to see our mother, and then the men, climb into a waiting car—a car that hadn't been there when we'd arrived. I started for the front door, but Jack grabbed my arm.

"No, it'll just get Mom more upset."

We watched out the window as the car drove off.

CHAPTER THREE

THE CAR TURNED THE CORNER, and it was gone. Our mother was gone. I looked over at Jack. He stood there, motionless, no expression on his face, staring out the window.

"Jack?"

He didn't answer. He didn't even turn in my direction or acknowledge that I'd spoken.

"Jack," I said louder. "What do we do?"

He turned to face me. "We eat."

"What?" I couldn't believe my ears.

"We eat." He turned and started for the kitchen.

For a while I just stood there, stunned, not moving. Finally I snapped to and hurried into the kitchen.

"How can you eat?"

"I'm hungry."

"How can you be hungry at a time like this?" I demanded.

"I was hungry two hours ago, so wouldn't it make sense that I'd be even hungrier now?" he asked as he reached into the cupboard and pulled out a jar of peanut butter.

"But ... but ... but after everything that happened ..."

"I'm still hungry. I have to eat so that I can think. I need my stomach full so my head can be clear."

He pulled a loaf of bread out of the breadbox and a knife out of the drawer and started to make a sandwich. "You want one?" he asked.

"No, of course I don't ..." My stomach was grumbling. "I guess so."

Jack finished up the first sandwich and then started to slather peanut butter on a second piece of bread. "Get the milk."

"Oh ... sure." I opened the fridge and grabbed the milk. I set it down on the table and then took two glasses out of the cupboard and filled them both to the top.

Jack brought over the sandwiches and put one on the table in front of me. We both sat down. I took a bite. It tasted good. Much better than a peanut butter sandwich should have tasted. Jack sat across the table from me. He was totally focused, working his way through his sandwich bite by bite, washing it down with the milk. Within thirty seconds the plate was empty and the glass was drained.

"What now?" I asked.

"Do you want another sandwich?"

"No. I want to know what we're going to do."

"We're going to think things through," he said. At least he was sounding like a sane person again. "Do you really think they have somebody inside the camp?"

"Could be. After all, remember what Bill told us about the type of people they train as spies," I said.

"What do you mean?"

"He said they don't just use soldiers to become spies. They use all sorts of people, people who have all sorts of different and strange skills. Safe-crackers, forgers, pickpockets and criminals of all kinds."

"That's right," Jack said. "And if one of those people training to be a spy used to work for those mobsters, then maybe he's passing on information."

"Who are those guys?"

"Isn't it obvious?" Jack asked.

"Well, criminals, right?"

"Not just any criminals. I figure they're part of the mob, organized criminals, the underworld."

"Like gangsters?" I asked.

"Yeah, gangsters."

"At least they're not Nazis."

"If they were we'd know where they stand. Mobsters are less predictable. I bet they'd even sell out to the Nazis if there was money to be made."

"Like the gold reserves of the Bank of England?" I asked.

Jack nodded.

"Either way, they must have somebody inside," I said. "How else would they know everything that they know?"

"I don't know … there could be other ways."

"Like what?"

"Like maybe they did get their information from inside the camp, but that doesn't mean they *still* have a contact inside."

"What do you mean by that?"

"Think about it. People move in and out of the camp all the time. They come in, get trained and leave."

"So you think whoever betrayed the information has gone?"

"Maybe. What information did he have about us?"

"He knew that Mom worked at Camp 30, and that we had to move to Bowmanville because of what had happened at Camp X, and he knew where we live," I said.

"Right, and that's all stuff somebody would know from a while ago. He didn't seem to know anything about the escape from Camp 30 or us being involved in it."

I hadn't thought about it, but he was right. They hadn't mentioned anything about any of that.

"But the two camps are separate, so why should a person from one place know about the other?" I asked.

"Because they're not separate, they're connected. Remember, the mail for Camp 30 is screened at Camp X. And who do you think was in charge of stopping the escape from Camp 30?" Jack asked.

"Yeah, that's right. I guess there really isn't much that happens around here about the war that doesn't go back to Camp X."

"Not much, and probably nothing that isn't known by Bill and *especially* by Little Bill."

"You're right," I admitted. "But maybe he knew about it but he figured there was no point in talking about it because what happened there doesn't matter. They only wanted to talk about Camp X because that's where the gold is."

"I don't think so. That guy was trying to impress us with what he knew, and if he knew more he would have said all of it."

"So … if whoever told them is gone from Camp X, then we could try and contact Bill, right?"

"Right. If we knew for sure."

"But we can't really know for sure, can we?" I asked.

"No, we can't, and because of that we can't take the risk. We have to assume that their inside guy might still be there, or that if they had one informant they might have a second now, or a third."

"Do you really think so?"

"I don't know what to think. I just know we can't take a chance with Mom's life. Until we know for sure, we have to act like everybody—except Bill and Little Bill—could be the snitch. We talk to nobody." He paused. "Nobody but Doris."

"Doris?" Doris was a secretary who worked with our mother at Camp 30. "Why would we contact Doris? How can she help us?"

"She can help us by telling them at Camp 30 that Mom is sick with the measles and she won't be in for the next few days. I'd better call her now."

"Why not tomorrow?"

"Because tomorrow we won't be here to call anybody."

"Why won't we be here?" I didn't know what he was going to say but I was pretty anxious about his answer.

"Because we're leaving tonight."

"Leaving for where?"

"Camp X."

CHAPTER FOUR

JACK HAD CALLED DORIS. She'd not only agreed to tell Colonel Armstrong that Mom was sick, she was also going to call our school and let them know that the two of us would be absent for the next few days. Jack told her that we were being picked up and driven to our grandmother's house in Whitby, and she was going to take care of all three of us until Mom got better. That wasn't quite the truth. Both our grandmothers were dead, we didn't know anybody who lived in Whitby, and nobody was going to be taking care of us or anything else. But we *were* going to Whitby.

"You ready to go?" Jack asked.

"I think so." I stuffed the box of cereal into my knapsack. "I just don't know why we have to go right now."

"First off, the sooner we get there the better."

"But couldn't we at least wait until morning?"

"No, we can't wait until morning because it's light in the morning. We have to get away from here without anybody seeing us. What if somebody—a teacher, a neighbour, somebody who knows Doris or somebody at Camp 30—sees us riding away on our bikes? Think about what that could lead to."

I didn't want to think about it. I knew there could be terrible consequences ... for us and for Mom. I looked up at the clock. It was just after midnight. Late enough that the streets and then the highway would be almost deserted.

"I have the sleeping bags and tent tied onto the bikes. Just think of this as a little camping trip. Nothing wrong with camping, is there?"

"I guess not."

"Did you get the flashlights?" Jack asked.

"Oops ... forgot." I ran across the kitchen and pulled them out of the drawer.

He shook his head. "Do you know how much trouble we would have been in without those? It would be almost impossible to pitch the tent in the dark without flashlights."

"I got 'em, so we're okay."

"Yeah, because I reminded you. Is there anything else I need to remind you to bring?" Jack asked.

"If I knew that, I wouldn't need you to remind me, would I?"

Jack walked away. I slung the knapsack onto my back. It was heavy, and some of the boxes and cans stuck into my back and ... Can opener. I was supposed to put a can opener in my bag. Casually I walked over and took the can opener out of the utensil drawer and slipped it into my pocket.

"Come on, let's get going!" Jack yelled from the other room.

As I turned I saw the slip of paper still on the table—the paper with the phone number we had to call. I grabbed it and stuffed it in my pocket.

"Before I lock the door, is there anything *else* you've forgotten?" Jack taunted.

"It's not like *you've* never forgotten anything before."

"Maybe before, but not tonight."

Dramatically, I reached into my pocket and pulled out the phone number. Jack's jaw dropped.

"I ... I ..."

"What would we have done without the telephone number? It isn't like we could ride back here and get it."

Jack didn't answer right away and I suddenly started to feel bad for what I'd said.

"You're right." Jack reached out and took the paper. "That was stupid, and we can't afford for anybody to be stupid ... especially me. I'm in charge, and I have to make sure everything goes right!"

He looked really angry and I didn't want that anger aimed at me. The stupid part wasn't him forgetting the phone number but me taunting Jack with the paper and— Suddenly he didn't look as angry as he did upset. I could swear that I almost saw tears forming in his eyes. He turned away. Now I was scared, more scared than if he had threatened to smack me. That happened on a regular basis, but seeing him in tears was really, really unusual.

"It's okay, Jack," I said softly.

"It's not okay," he said through gritted teeth, without turning around. "I can't make any mistakes. None."

"It's going to be all right. It's taken care of," I said reassuringly.

"But it almost wasn't. It's up to me to make sure that everything works."

I thought about Jack and what he did around the house. With Dad off fighting in Africa and Mom working at Camp 30, it often felt like Jack was in charge, like he wasn't my older brother but almost a parent. Jack had been the one who had shouldered so much responsibility for me and for everything else, and now he must have felt like it was all up to him to take care of what was happening with Mom.

"Look, Jack, it isn't just you. It's you and me ... together, like a team."

"Yeah, like having you help is supposed to be reassuring to me," he huffed.

"It should be. You think you could have gotten us through all that we've gone through without my help, without my ideas? Who got free when we were tied up in that deserted farmhouse? Who drove the jeep when your arm was broken? Who figured out how to trick those soldiers? I may be your little brother, but I'm not your *stupid* little brother. We can do this. Together, we can do it."

Jack spun around to face me. I half expected him to tell me to shut up and maybe even give me a poke in the shoulder. Instead he looked me square in the eyes.

"You weren't *completely* useless."

That was as close as Jack ever came to giving me a compliment.

"Okay," he said, "let's get going."

"Something's coming!" Jack yelled.

I saw the headlights as well, way up ahead. I swerved off the road and as far off onto the gravel shoulder as I could get. I jumped off the bike and dropped to the ground, hiding partially behind it and partially in the ditch. The car—I could now tell from the size and shape it was a car—got closer and closer. By the sound of the engine it was obvious that it was really flying. The headlights swept forward and then for a split second washed over me. I felt open and exposed and visible, and then they were gone, and I was safely hidden in the dark.

I got up and picked up my bike. Jack, just ahead, did the same thing. We mounted up and started pedalling again. We had done this two dozen times in

the past two hours. Highway 2 was the only road we
knew of to get from Bowmanville to Whitby, and
since it was a major route we kept hitting traffic, in
spite of the fact that it was the middle of the night.
Even though we'd been riding for close to two hours
and were well away from anybody who might know
us in Bowmanville, we still had to scramble into the
ditch with each passing vehicle. We couldn't risk
being seen. What if it was a police car? How would we
explain being out on our bikes in the middle of the
night, and what if the copper wanted to talk to our
mother? We just couldn't risk it.

The sweat I was working up riding kept getting
sucked away by the cold air. The September days were
still warm but the nights were cold, and that chill
seeped right through my windbreaker. I'd welcome
the warmth of the first light of morning, but that was
still over three hours away.

I was feeling more and more tired. The first twenty
minutes of the trip hadn't been so bad. We'd been full
of energy and adrenalin, and I'd tried to convince
myself it was a game. Like hide-and-go-seek or
soldiers-and-spies. Actually, we *were* playing spies.
We'd skirted around Bowmanville without running
into anybody or anything. The whole town had been
tucked into bed. We'd passed a few houses that had
lights on but those were the only signs of wakefulness
we'd seen in the whole town.

"How much farther do you think we have to go?" I called out to Jack.

"Quit complaining!" Jack yelled back over his shoulder.

I pedalled harder until I was right beside him. "I'm not complaining, I just want to know."

"We've been riding for about two hours and we've gone about twenty-five miles."

"I know how long we've been riding. I want to know how much *longer* we have to ride."

"Didn't you see the sign back there? The one that said 'Oshawa 3 miles'?"

"I didn't see anything."

"That was a mile ago. Oshawa is just up ahead. Whitby is the next town after that and the camp is between the two."

"So not that much longer."

"No. I'm just worried about going through Oshawa. It's big and we're going to be passing a lot of houses, and maybe a lot of cars, too. I'm still worried about us getting stopped by the police."

I dropped back behind Jack. I should have figured we were getting closer to something. There were more and more houses plopped down along the road, but thank goodness there were still no signs of life within them. Lights were out, shades were drawn, and everybody was surely asleep inside, tucked into bed.

I couldn't help thinking about my bed, snuggling in under the covers, pulling the pillow up so it partially covered my face and kept me warm, and Mom would be just down the hall and ... Where was she now, how was she doing, was she okay or ...? I couldn't let my mind go there. I couldn't afford to lose focus, because the only way we had to help her was to stay alert.

Suddenly a car pulled out from one of the driveways and its headlights swept over us before we had a chance to react. The car raced by, a little gust of wind hitting me. I looked over my shoulder. It didn't slow down, just kept on going, the tail lights getting smaller and smaller, until it followed the road around a bend and was gone.

There could be no question that we'd been seen by whoever was in the car, but maybe they wouldn't know what to do—or if they should do anything at all—about two kids out on their bikes in the middle of the night. We had to be more careful.

The road remained empty but the scenery started to change. The ditches at the side of the road gave way to wide, gravel shoulders, and the houses were now much closer to the road and closer together. There'd be almost no place to hide if another car came along. Even more troubling, up ahead, the darkness was replaced by the glow of street lights—lights marking the centre of Oshawa.

"Should we try to find a way around it?" I called out to Jack.

"I don't know another way. Do you?" he yelled back.

"No, but what if somebody sees us?"

"I hope they'll just do what that car did and ignore us. We have to bike harder ... faster," Jack yelled over his shoulder.

Jack doubled his pace and I struggled to keep up with him, my legs burning and my knees aching. Soon the gravel shoulders became sidewalks and the houses became storefronts. Our images were reflected off the darkened windows. This was eerie. Pedalling through the middle of the town, all the stores closed and locked up, the lights out, sidewalks and roads deserted, the only sound my bike chain clicking. It was like we were the only people in the world and—Suddenly the headlights of a car parked beside the road came on, and the illusion was gone.

"Just keep pedalling," Jack said. "Just ignore it and—"

Flashing red lights came pulsing from the top—it was a police car!

CHAPTER FIVE

THE DOOR OF THE CAR OPENED, and a large, uniformed police officer climbed out. One of his hands was held high in the air, ordering us to pull over. There was no place to hide and no way to run. My gut wanted to try to get away anyway, take off, race off, but my head knew better. We skidded to a stop in front of him and climbed off our bikes.

"Awful late to be out for a bike ride, isn't it, boys?" he asked.

"Not late. Early," Jack said. "We're just heading home. Our mother doesn't expect us until tomorrow afternoon, but we thought we'd get there and have breakfast waiting for her—it's her birthday."

"That would be a mighty nice surprise. So she doesn't know you're coming, that you're out in the middle of the night, is that what you're saying?"

"No, sir," Jack said, "but our grandma knows—that's where we were staying, at her place."

"Interesting, because judging from the gear you have on your bikes it looks more like you were camping out somewhere."

"We were," I said. "At our grandma's place. Her house isn't that big and the weather was so great and we like camping."

"You sure you two boys aren't running away from home?"

"Us?" I asked, sounding genuinely surprised. "We'd *never* run away from home."

"All this is just our camping gear," Jack said. "Do you want to ask our grandma?"

I tried to hide my surprise at his question—was he trying to get us caught?

"That might be a fine idea. Just give me her phone number and I'll radio it in and have somebody give her a call."

"That wouldn't work," Jack said. "She's pretty deaf and she takes her hearing aid out at night. You could just drive us there."

The officer shrugged. "Nothing better to do. Where does she live?"

"In Bowmanville," Jack said.

Now I knew what he was doing. "Yeah, the *far* side of Bowmanville."

"You rode all the way from Bowmanville in the middle of the night?"

"It's not that far, and it's better to travel at night because it's cooler and the road is almost empty," Jack said.

"No argument about that."

"So, should we get in?" Jack asked, pointing at the car.

"'Fraid not. I can't be driving that far. I'm the only officer on duty tonight and I can't leave the whole town unpatrolled. So where is your home? Where are you riding *to*?"

"We're not far now. We live in Whitby," Jack said.

"What's your address?" the officer asked.

I waited for Jack to answer and he waited for me. Finally Jack spoke up.

"This is going to sound stupid," he said, "but we just moved there a month ago so I don't know our actual address."

"But we know *where* it is," I added. "It's just that they haven't even put up numbers on some of the houses because they built so many—it's a new house."

"A tiny house," Jack said.

"A lot smaller than our farm," I said. "We had to move because our mother is working in Ajax at the munitions plant … she couldn't work the farm alone because our dad enlisted. He's fighting with the St. Patrick's Regiment in Africa."

I'd learned that it usually helped to mention that our father was a solider.

"Lots of people are moving to this area to get work." He pulled a notepad out of his shirt pocket and flipped it open. "I'd better take down your names."

I looked at Jack. What were we going to tell him?

"I'm Jack and this is my brother George."

"Last name?"

"Smith," I said, before Jack could answer.

"Smith … seems like everybody I run into is named Smith or Jones. Do either of you boys have identification on you?"

I shook my head.

"I'd have a driver's licence if I was old enough," Jack said.

The cop shook his head slowly. "That's what I thought. How about if we put your bikes in the trunk of my patrol car and I'll drive you home."

"I thought you couldn't leave the town," I said.

"Bowmanville is pretty far. Whitby is just a stone's throw away," he explained.

"We don't want to put you to any trouble. We'll just ride … it won't take long."

"No trouble."

He reached down and put a hand on my bike. Before I could even react he started to roll it toward the car. I looked over at Jack, pleading with my eyes for an answer. He shrugged. The officer opened the trunk of the car and lifted my bike in. Jack walked his bike over and the officer did the same with his. He tried to close the lid but he couldn't. He shifted the bikes around, tried again and the lid closed.

"How about you two ride up front," he said.

He climbed in on his side and we got in on the

passenger side. He started the car and pulled away from the curb.

We drove along in silence at first, cruising through the downtown of Oshawa before heading into more-open space.

"This is a lot easier than riding your bikes," he pointed out.

"And a lot faster," Jack said. "Thanks for doing this."

"No problem. You two ever been in a police car before?" he asked.

"Lots of times," I said.

"You have?" He sounded surprised. Probably as surprised as Jack was with my answer.

"Yeah, our uncle has driven us in his car. You might know him. He's the Chief of Police in Whitby."

"You're related to Chief Smith?" he asked, sounding pleasantly surprised.

"He's our father's brother," I lied. We'd got to know Chief Smith when we lived in Whitby. He was one of the few people who knew that we were involved with Camp X.

"Do you know him?" Jack asked.

"I know him well. He's a hell ... I mean, a *heck* of a good guy."

"He is," I said. "Everybody thinks because he's so big and scary-looking that he must be mean, but we know he's really just a softy."

"The turn is just up ahead," Jack said.

The car slowed down and he made the turn off the highway. Jack was directing him to our old house—the place we lived when we did live in Whitby.

"Now turn here," Jack directed. "We're the fourth house."

The officer pulled the car over to the side of the road, right in front of our old house. It was dark. All the houses were dark. There was no sign of life anywhere on the street. We climbed out of the car and circled around to the trunk. The officer opened it and removed first Jack's bike and then mine.

"Thanks a lot. And when we talk to our uncle, who should we say helped us?" I asked.

"Fred Johnson," he said.

"Thanks a lot, Mr. Johnson … I mean, Officer Johnson," Jack said.

"That's okay, boys. You just get yourselves inside and get a little sleep."

"Thanks a lot and good night," I said.

Jack and I took our bikes and started to walk toward the house.

"Walk slowly," Jack whispered. "Maybe he'll drive away."

I didn't dare look over my shoulder but I heard the car door slam. Unfortunately I didn't hear the engine start. We leaned our bikes against the porch.

"He isn't leaving," I hissed.

We walked onto the porch. We turned around. In the dim light I could see Officer Johnson sitting in the car, behind the wheel, watching, waiting to make sure we got in safely. Jack waved and I did the same. He still didn't move.

"What now?" I asked.

"We hope the door isn't locked," Jack said.

He turned the knob and the door opened. Jack turned around one more time, waved to Officer Johnson, and walked in. I was right behind him. Jack closed the door as silently as possible and we stood just inside, in the pitch-black in somebody else's house! My knees were shaking, I was afraid to move, afraid to breathe. Somewhere in the darkness—probably in beds in the rooms where our mother or Jack and I used to sleep—were people. What if they heard us? What if they came out and discovered us in their living room?

From outside I heard the sound of a car starting. Jack shifted over a few feet and peeked out through the window. There was a flash of lights—they must have been the headlights of the car. They swept through the window and then were gone, leaving us in the dark again.

Jack grabbed my hand and pulled me forward, opening the door. We rushed out, closed the door behind us, grabbed our bikes and pedalled off as fast as our legs could make us go.

CHAPTER SIX

I OPENED MY EYES and then partially shielded them with my hand to block out the brilliant sunlight. I didn't know what time it was, but the sun was already pretty high in the sky—high enough to heat up our little tent. The top of the tent sagged dangerously low, so low that it looked like the whole thing might collapse. No surprise there. Jack had made us pitch the tent in the dark. He wouldn't use the flashlights—the flashlights that he'd given me a hard time about almost forgetting. He said he didn't want to risk some-body's seeing the lights flashing around in the dark and coming to investigate. Like *that* would have happened.

From our old house, we'd taken our bikes along the familiar roads that got us close to the camp perimeter. After that we had to push our bikes, stumbling through the forest, until we were closer to the camp, but far enough from the road that Jack was satisfied no one would see us. It was tough going in the dark, and I got more than a few branches in my face, but we finally stopped at a little clearing … a little clearing a full mile above the northern boundary of Camp X.

I shifted my body over to the side to try to get away from a rock that had forged a little dent in my back. That worked—sort of. Now I had another rock digging into a different part of my back. If we'd used the flashlights we could have cleared the ground before we set up.

Maybe this was my signal to get up—a sore back and a grumbly stomach. I was hungry. In fact, I was so hungry that I could almost imagine the smell of bacon floating through the air. I inhaled deeply. Wait a second ... that wasn't my imagination, I *could* smell bacon cooking.

I sat up. Jack's sleeping bag was empty. I flopped out of mine and crawled over to the flap and peeked out. Jack was squatting by a small fire, a frying pan in one hand and a spatula in the other.

"Smells good," I said.

He turned around. "It does. I bet it'll taste even better."

"I'm sure it will, because food always tastes best when you're hungry, and I'm so hungry I could eat a—"

"What makes you think you're getting any of this?" he asked. "You want breakfast, you should make yourself something."

"That's not fair!"

Jack chuckled. "Maybe you can have a little. Grab a plate."

I stumbled out of the tent, practically falling flat on my face before I got to my feet. There were two plates sitting on the ground beside Jack and I grabbed one. The frying pan was filled with four eggs—two over hard, the way I liked them—and eight or ten strips of bacon. Obviously Jack had been planning on feeding me from the start.

"Notice how the fire is hardly making any smoke at all?" Jack asked.

I hadn't until he mentioned it. There was just a little smoke coming from the flames, and it disappeared without a trace after rising a few feet into the air.

"I used really dry sticks. Smoke is from the moisture caught in the wood. I didn't want any smoke because it could draw attention to us."

"Smart, but aren't you worried about the smell of the bacon? That's what caught *my* attention."

"I hadn't thought about that—do you think somebody might notice?" he asked. He sounded worried.

"There's nobody around for a mile, and even if they did smell something, what would they think—that somebody was making breakfast?"

"I guess you're right."

Jack took the spatula and put four pieces of bacon and the two over-hard eggs onto my plate. He scooped the rest onto his.

I picked up one of the pieces of hot bacon with my fingers and popped it into my mouth. Jack handed me a fork and then sat down on the edge of a fallen log. I sat down beside him.

"This is really good," I said.

"Like you said, that just means you're really hungry."

"Probably from all that bike riding … although I would have been happier if we could have made it the whole way on our bikes and stayed out of the police car," I said.

"Me too." He stuffed a piece of bacon in his mouth. "That was pretty quick about us being related to Chief Smith. Probably why he gave us a break. How did you think of that?"

"It just sort of came to me after I lied about our last name," I said.

"That was pretty smart too. I wish I hadn't told him our real first names."

I shrugged. "It doesn't matter. So what if he has our first names?"

"Probably means nothing, I guess. But that's going to be one strange conversation when he mentions meeting us to Chief Smith."

I hadn't thought of that. "Maybe they don't talk. They don't even work for the same police department."

"Maybe they don't talk very often, but I bet they do talk, or they talk to people who talk to each other.

It'll get back to him eventually," Jack said.

"Even if it does, he only has our first names. There have to be lots of boys named Jack and George," I reasoned.

"Who lived in our old house, the one that we were driven to?"

All at once the food that had tasted so good going down started to form a lump in my stomach.

"But I bet you it won't happen in the next few days," Jack said. "It might not even happen in the next few months. And even if they talk later and they make the connection, what's Chief Smith gonna do? He doesn't even know where we live now."

He was right, and that was reassuring.

"It's funny, though," Jack said. "I was thinking about the people in Whitby who knew about us, and besides the people at Camp X there is only one other person—Chief Smith."

"I hadn't thought about that, but he did know a lot, didn't he?"

"Well, Bill had to tell Chief Smith about the stuff that happened so he'd go along with the cover story to explain how we ended up in the hospital, and how Mr. Krum was supposedly killed in a car crash," Jack said.

"But you don't think he's the one who told those criminals about us, do you?" I asked.

"Who knows?"

"Wouldn't it be funny if the guy who betrayed us was the guy whose name got us out of that tight spot last night?" I said.

"'Funny' isn't the word that comes to my mind," Jack said. "I was thinking about betrayal. Us betraying Camp X." Jack didn't continue his thought right away. He looked as though all he was thinking about was his breakfast. "We signed the Official Secrets Act, we took an oath, and now look at us," he finally said.

"We didn't really tell those guys anything," I argued.

"Maybe we didn't, but think about what we're doing now. We're going to bring some criminals into the camp so that they can steal gold. It doesn't matter what we say or don't say, it's what we're planning on *doing*."

"What choice do we have?" I asked.

"None. You just gotta know that if they catch us we're in big trouble. We might go to jail. We might get shot. That's what they do to traitors."

"But we're not traitors!" I protested. "Well ... not really. We're just going to help them take a little gold so that we can get our mother back."

"Still, we'd better not get caught ... not just because of what would happen to us, but what would happen to Mom."

"I don't care what happens to us," I said.

"You'd better. If we get caught, who do you think is going to save her?"

A chill went up my spine. He was right. We couldn't get caught. We *couldn't*!

"This isn't a game, George. This isn't some kind of fun camping trip. Now, how about you pack up the tent and I'll put out the fire and clean up out here. Then we'd better get going."

It didn't take long to bundle up the camping gear. I stashed it with our bikes, which were hidden beneath some branches we'd cut down the night before. Jack made sure the fire was out, and then he tried to make it look like there'd never been a fire there to begin with. Together, we did our best to remove every trace of the whole campsite.

Finally we were ready to find our way back to Camp X. Jack led because he knew what he was doing and where he was going. I didn't need to know anything. I just had to follow. Of course that didn't mean I wasn't watching and listening and thinking.

We made our way out of the woods and crossed through an abandoned field. I could now see the railroad embankment up ahead. That was the northern boundary of the camp.

"Do we climb up and get into the camp here?" I asked.

"Not yet, and not here."

We walked along in the shadow of the embankment.

"I'm still not sure what we're doing," I said.

"We're scouting. We have to try to see if anything has changed since we were last here. You know, extra security or anything. We have to find the best way in."

"It just seems like another chance for us to get caught."

"We might be seen, but that doesn't mean we'll be caught," Jack said. "As long as it's just the two of us, even if we're seen we can run and the guards will probably just let us go. They'll think it's only a couple of local kids who've wandered by. I bet that happens all the time. But if we get caught looking around with those men, then the guards aren't going to laugh it off. They're going to come after us."

"I guess you're right."

"Of *course* I'm right. Now keep your mouth shut and your ears and eyes open."

I wasn't going to argue, because that had been my plan anyway.

"There's the trestle!" I said, pointing up ahead. The embankment trailed off and was replaced by a high wooden railroad bridge crossing Corbett's Creek.

"They said the gold was being stored in the caves down by the lake so I thought the creek would probably be the best way in. It worked before," Jack said.

"If they haven't put more guards on it since we went in that way the last time."

"That's what we're here to find out," Jack explained. He started up the side of the embankment, and I started after him. Stones and cinders shifted under my feet as I struggled to climb. I dropped to all fours, using my hands to get me to the top. By then Jack was standing in the middle of the tracks. I looked up and down the line. There was nothing coming in either direction. I stepped over the first rail and stood beside him. Suddenly he got down on his knees and leaned his head against one of the rails.

"What are you doing?"

"Listening for oncoming trains."

"You can hear a train?" I asked anxiously.

"I can't hear anything ... which means we can cross the trestle."

"What?"

"We have to cross the trestle to get to the other side of the creek."

"But why do we have to cross? The camp is on *this* side of the creek."

"That's why we have to cross. Even if somebody does see us they won't think anything about it if we're not actually on the grounds of the camp."

Jack started down the tracks toward the trestle and again I trailed after him. As he started to move across the bridge I stopped and studied it. It was long and looked to be pretty high in the middle.

"You coming?" Jack yelled.

I didn't like heights and I didn't think this was such a smart idea, but what choice did I have? Slowly I started across the trestle. Within a dozen steps the ground underneath the track bed dropped away. Now it was just the rails, held together by the wooden ties and nothing but open air in between. Carefully I took a step to the next tie. They were wide, but not as wide as the gaps between them—gaps that were certainly big enough to let me fall through. I took another step, and then another. With each step the ground was falling farther and farther away. Just how far down would the creek be when I was in the middle?

"Hurry up!" Jack hissed at me.

I looked up. He was already standing on the far side.

"Do you want somebody to see you?" he demanded.

"I'm hurrying as fast as I can," I said. I dropped my eyes back to my feet. I stepped onto the next tie, first with one foot and then the other. I did the same thing again, and then again, and then again. Between the ties I could see the creek flowing below. It was a strange effect, the water rushing by underneath from right to left while I was moving forward. It made it feel like the bridge itself was moving … like my stomach was moving.

"George!" Jack hissed. "I think I hear a train."

My head jerked up. Anxiously I looked beyond Jack and along the tracks. I didn't see anything. I looked back over my shoulder. Nothing. I didn't see anything … I didn't hear anything … at least I didn't think so.

"Hurry up!"

I looked down at the next tie. I stepped onto it. Rather than bring my other foot forward onto that tie I stepped straight to the next. Maybe I didn't have time to take baby steps. I kept on taking the ties one at a time, one after the other. There couldn't be that many more now. I could see that the ground was starting to rise to meet the rails again. As the ground got closer I got more confident and started to move faster and faster. I stopped when I reached Jack's side and waited for the pounding in my chest to settle down.

"Took you long enough."

"But I'm here," I said, looking down the tracks. "So where's the train?"

Jack smirked. "I didn't really hear one, but I thought you needed a little encouragement."

He had put me through all that for nothing? "You know, Jack, sometimes you're a real—" I stopped myself mid-sentence. I heard something. Jack turned around.

Then we both saw it. Up the tracks, steaming toward us, was a train! It was a fair way down the tracks but it was moving incredibly quickly for something that big. I was mesmerized by it.

Jack grabbed my arm and yanked me off the tracks! We plunged, feet first, down the embankment, skidding, sending an avalanche of cinders and stones down before us. I hit the bottom and tumbled forward, landing face first in a heap. I turned to look up at the engine and there was a blast of air and my face was pummelled with a shower of grit and cinders. The ground underneath me was shaking. I watched, my eyes partially shielded by a hand, as car after car thundered by. It was a long, long train. Finally the caboose swished past, and the shaking and the sound got softer and softer until both were gone completely.

"You planning on lying there all day?" Jack asked.

Embarrassed, I got to my feet and brushed myself off.

"Lucky thing I lied to you to get you moving," Jack said. "If I hadn't, you'd be a stain on the tracks right about now."

A little shiver went up my spine. He was probably right. If I hadn't started to move faster I would have still been on the trestle when I saw the train, and if I'd frozen or fallen or—

"You can always count on me," Jack said. "At least, count on me to give you a hard time. Come on, let's get moving."

CHAPTER SEVEN

JACK PICKED UP THE RECEIVER of the telephone.
We were at a pay phone at the side of a little gas
station on the highway. It was the first phone we'd
been able to find. Jack held the phone so I could listen
in to the conversation. He dialled zero and the phone
started to ring.

"Operator," a nasally voice sang out.

"Yeah … hi … we have to make a call … a collect
call."

"What is the number?" she asked.

Jack held the phone against his shoulder and
unfolded the paper. He read out the numbers.

"And who should I say is calling?" the operator
asked.

"Jack … Jack Braun."

"Hold please, Mr. Braun." The line suddenly went
silent.

"Let me do all the talking," Jack said.

I nodded my head.

"They have accepted the charges," the operator
said. "I'm connecting the call."

There was a click. "Hello?" Jack said.

"Hello," came a voice—the familiar voice of that man. "Is that you, Jack?"

"It's me."

"I didn't expect to hear from you so soon. It's been less than twenty-four hours, and I gave you three days."

"You want the gold and we want our mother. There was no point in waiting any longer than we had to," Jack said.

We did want her back as soon as possible. We also knew that the more we probed the camp the greater the chance we would get caught. We'd travelled the length of the creek, right down to the lake, and it was unguarded. The creek was still the best choice, and there was no point in looking any farther.

"So, I'm assuming that you've found a way in."

"We know how to do it."

"Excellent. Where shall I have my men meet you?" he asked.

"We're not meeting them anywhere until we know our mother is safe," Jack said.

"She's safe."

"We want to talk to her."

"You'll be able to talk to her as soon as you get here with the gold."

"We're not meeting your men and we're not bringing you any gold until we know that she's okay," Jack insisted.

"You're not in any position to be dictating terms to me," the man said, his voice now ominously angry.

"That depends on how much you want the gold," Jack pointed out.

"And that depends on whether or not you ever want to see your mother alive again," he threatened.

"Until we talk to her, we don't even know that she still *is* alive."

The man started to chuckle. His laughter was even more frightening. "Hang on," he said.

Jack slipped his hand over the mouthpiece. "I think he's gone to get her."

Seconds turned to a full minute, and I was starting to feel more and more anxious.

"Hello, Jack?"

"Mom!" we both yelled out.

"George, are you there too?"

"We're both here. Are you okay?" Jack asked.

"I'm fine."

"They haven't hurt you, have they?" Jack asked.

"No. They've been treating me well … as well as you can treat a prisoner. Are you boys all right?"

"We're fine. We'll be there by tomorrow."

"Boys, you can't risk—"

"Satisfied?" the man said, his voice replacing our mother's. "She's fine, and she'll stay fine as long as you continue to co-operate. Now, where and when do my men meet you?"

"They should come along Highway 2 until they hit Corbett's Creek. It's just outside of Whitby before you come to Oshawa. There's a spot for them to pull off the road just east of the creek. They need to be there by seven o'clock. Can they do that?"

"That's no problem."

"And they need to bring a rubber raft big enough to hold four people."

"That might be a little more difficult to come by," he said.

"Difficult or impossible?" Jack asked.

"We'll arrange it. My men will be there at seven. Anything else?" he asked.

"Nothing. Except I have a question."

"Go ahead."

"These two guys you're sending, how do we know that they can be trusted?"

"You have nothing to worry about, they'll cooperate with you fully."

"No," Jack said. "I mean, how do you know *you* can trust them? How do you know they won't just get the gold and then take off, leaving all of us high and dry?"

The man laughed. "No worries."

"Yeah, I know you're saying that, but I don't want to go to all the risk of getting the gold out and then have these guys take off. How do I know they're trustworthy?"

"You know for the same reason we can trust you to do what we agreed," he said.

For a second I wondered if that meant that he had *their* mothers hostage, but I knew that was stupid.

"You're to be trusted because a member of your family is dependent on you being trustworthy," he explained. "These two men are family."

"They're your cousins or something?" Jack asked.

The three of them looked nothing alike, so I couldn't imagine them being related.

"Not cousins," he said. "More like brothers. We're a family business. Everybody in the organization has taken an oath, and we would never turn our backs on our brothers. I would trust these two with my life, so you should trust them too." He paused and then chuckled slightly. "Actually, you *are* trusting them with your lives, and your mother's."

He was right, and that thought made me feel shivery all over.

"Besides, nobody would ever double-cross me," he said. "If they even tried I would hunt them down like dogs and kill them, slowly and painfully."

I knew that threat was aimed at us.

"And one more thing," Jack said. "Have them dress like they're going fishing and bring along fishing rods and a tackle box and bait."

"Very smart. That way if somebody sees you they'll think you're just a couple of kids with their fathers out on a little fishing trip. My compliments. You boys have really thought this through. I had my doubts at first," he said, "but I think if anybody can pull it off, you two can."

"We'll hold up our end of the bargain. You just keep yours."

"My word is as good as gold … as good as the gold you're going to be bringing to me. Now, is there anything else?"

"Nothing. We'll be there." Jack hung up the phone.

I tilted my head to the side so I could see Jack's watch. It was a few minutes before seven. We were hidden behind some bushes, close enough to see the road but far enough not to be seen by anybody driving by. It was still early enough in the evening for the road to be well travelled. We'd seen lots of cars and a number of big trucks—some of them probably coming from the DIL munitions plant in Ajax, just down the road. That was where our mother used to work. It always made us nervous that she was working in the middle of a factory filled with explosives.

We were happier when she started working at Camp 30—not that being just a couple of fences away from five hundred German prisoners-of-war was that much better. Now, I just wished she were working at the factory instead of being where she was tonight.

"They should be here by now," I whispered.

"It's just a minute past seven. They'll be coming. They want the gold. It only seems like they're late because we've been waiting so long."

Jack had made us come to the meeting stop over an hour before the agreed time. He said he wanted to be in a place where he could watch things in case they were going to try to pull a fast one on us, maybe bring along extra people or something like that. I hated waiting but I knew that it was the smart thing to do. From where we were we could see everything that was coming or going along the road for half a mile in each direction. The only way somebody could come up on us was from behind, and that wouldn't work. First off, since we were in position, staying quiet, nobody would even know where we were to sneak up on us. And second, anybody coming through the woods would make enough noise for us to hear them approaching. We were safe.

"I've been thinking about how we have to act around these guys," Jack said quietly.

"I'll try to be calm."

"No, I was thinking you should act scared."

"Believe me, I won't have to *act* scared."

Jack smiled.

"I can do it. I just don't understand. Why do you want me to act that way?"

"You know how when a duck is sitting on the water it looks really calm but its legs are moving really fast?"

"Um, yeah, I guess, but what has that got to do with us?"

"We have to be the opposite of that duck. We have to be calm underneath, thinking things through, but on the surface we have to appear to be nervous, unsure, to throw them off. We want them to see us as just a couple of stupid kids who don't know anything, who they don't have to worry about."

"And while we're acting scared on the surface, we're thinking, and they won't realize we're thinking."

"They'll underestimate us," Jack said. "It's just like Bill once told us: when they train spies they tell them to put on a big smile, or even act like they're simple or stupid, so that nobody suspects them."

"That all makes sense. I just wish they'd get here."

"We didn't give them much time," Jack added.

"All part of the plan."

That was my idea. I figured if they only had a few hours to get here, they wouldn't have enough time to plan something. All they could do was react to what we told them to do.

"They might have had trouble getting the raft," Jack suggested.

"Maybe. Speaking of the raft, we have to be sure to put ashore before we get to the waterfall," I said.

The creek had a sudden six-foot drop about half a mile past the trestle.

"Oh, yeah, I forgot to mention that part of my plan," Jack said. "We're going over the waterfall."

"What!" I exclaimed.

"Yeah. I figure if we go over the waterfall we'll all end up in the drink, and that would be good."

"How would that be good?" I asked.

"Because both of those guys are going to be packing heat, and I read that guns that get wet don't work," he explained.

"They don't?"

"Nope. I read that someplace. We want to get the gold out but we don't want them to kill anybody."

"That makes sense. I'm just not looking forward to going over those falls again."

The first time we'd gone down that way—while drifting on inflated inner tubes—we hadn't known about the waterfall. We'd gone flying over, plunging beneath the water in the pool at the bottom before breaking the surface and dragging ourselves to shore. That was one of the scariest moments of my life ... up until then, anyway. There had been lots worse since, and I had a nasty feeling there were lots more still to come.

"The other reason I want to travel by raft is so that we can see if we're being followed," Jack said.

"Followed by who?"

"By some more mobsters. It's important to know how many of them we're dealing with. I figure we stop before we hit the trestle, maybe hide under the branches of that big willow tree, just float there. We can tell them we have to wait to see if there are any guards watching from the trestle."

"I've never seen a guard on the trestle before," I said.

"Neither have I, but they don't know that. Then if somebody is following us they'll drift right into us. Does that make sense?"

"That's good thinking."

"Somebody's got to use their head for more than just holding a hat. I only wish I had all the rest of it worked out."

"I've been thinking about the rest of it too."

"And?"

"Well, even if this all works, what's to stop them from simply taking the gold and killing us and Mom?"

"I thought about that. That's not going to happen."

"But won't they be worried about us telling some-body what happened, you know, turning them in?"

"They probably figure that everybody is like them and we'll take the money and just shut up. They don't think that we'd squeal on them, because it would get us in hot water."

"I don't know," I said. "They have to be thinking about just keeping all the gold and getting rid of the witnesses."

Jack shook his head slowly. "You could be right. Maybe I can come up with another way—there's always another way."

I let out a big sigh. "Even if this all works, even if we do walk away with our mother and a lot of money, it's still wrong."

"You think I don't know that?" Jack snapped. "But what choice do we have?"

I shook my head. "None. We have to help them get the gold and get our mom back. We have no choice about that. Not now. But we *do* have a choice later on."

"Go on," Jack said.

"After we're all free, then we could go to Bill and tell him what happened."

Jack didn't answer.

"We could tell them about stealing the gold and how we really didn't have any choice, it was like a gun was being held to our heads—our mother's head—and then we could give him whatever information we have about the criminals and they could catch them."

"They could, but they'd already have half the gang. Us."

"Us?"

"It won't matter why we did what we did. We still did it. We still violated the Official Secrets Act. We still betrayed our country. They could still put us in jail or shoot us."

"And if they did, could you blame them? We're putting our lives above our country."

"Not *our* lives. Our *mother's* life."

"Makes no difference why you betray your country. We'd be punished, that's for sure."

"Are you saying we shouldn't tell Bill, that if we get away with it we should just stay quiet?" I asked.

Jack shook his head. "I was thinking about what Dad would want us to do."

"I know what he'd want us to do," I said.

"Me too. We'll contact Bill. We're doing something wrong so we have to take our punishment like men. We'll do what we have to do … and then, they'll do what they have to do to us."

CHAPTER EIGHT

"WHAT TIME IS IT NOW?" I asked Jack.

"About two minutes later than the last time you asked."

That made it about twenty-five after seven. Twenty-five minutes later than the time they should have been there.

"What do you think is keeping them?"

"What do I look like, a fortune teller?"

"Do you think they're going to come?"

"Of course. They want that gold, and they can't get it unless they do what we told them to do."

He was right. There was no reason to believe they weren't going to show up. They'd probably just had some trouble finding the raft, or maybe they'd got lost or—

"Look," I said.

A car had just come into view. It was big and black and looked a little like the car the mobsters had been driving. As it closed in I could see it was a beat-up old black sedan, not as fancy as theirs. It hit the bridge and kept going. I watched until it reached the bend in the road and disappeared.

"There's another one!" I exclaimed. "No ... wait ... it's just a truck."

A grey panel truck came lumbering along the road. Its gears made a grinding sound as it shifted and started to slow down. I heard the sound of gravel under its wheels at the same instant it started to pull off to the side of the road. It came to a stop just beside the bridge—just to the east side of the bridge.

"Do you think?" Jack asked.

In answer to his question the passenger door opened and a man—a big man—wearing a big, dressy overcoat and a fedora climbed out. Yeah, it was them.

"Is that his idea of how fishermen dress?" Jack asked.

"I guess it depends on what you're fishing for."

"You wait here and I'll go and talk to them." Jack started to get up.

I grabbed his arm. "No, it should be me who goes."

"No way. I'm the one who needs to talk to them in case they try something fishy."

"That's why it should be me," I argued. "If they try anything, we need you free to do something about it ... right?"

He didn't answer right away, which meant he was actually thinking about what I'd said. "I don't like it, but I guess you're right. I'll cover you from here."

"That would mean a lot more if you had a gun."

"It would. And go that way," he said, pointing away from the van. "We don't want them to know where you came from or where I'm hiding. Come at them from the other side of the road."

On all fours I crawled away, keeping my head below the bushes. The land dropped away and I was hidden from view. Cautiously, I moved along the edge of the creek. They were parked far enough from the bridge that they couldn't see me. I crept along the banks, moving slowly and quietly. Finally, sheltered by the abutment, I scurried under the bridge. It was instantly cooler, and I couldn't help but think how cold it was going to be when we went over the waterfall and got soaking wet. I picked out my steps carefully, moving from rock to rock to avoid getting a soaker.

I cleared the bridge and then came up the bank. I used a line of bushes to shelter me as I moved away from the creek. I stopped. Standing there, I was completely hidden from their view. Safe. If I just stayed there they'd never see me. I couldn't help but think about how tempting that was, and that this was probably the last time I was going to be safe for a long time. I didn't want to move but I knew I had to. I took a couple of deep breaths to steady myself, to calm down and try to stop my knees from shaking. I was going to act scared but I didn't want to let them know I was really terrified. Okay, it was time. I looked up and down the road. There were no other vehicles in sight.

I came out of the bushes, waving my hands. "Hey!"

They circled to the front of the van.

"Get in and follow me!" I yelled.

I started jogging down the road. I didn't look back but I heard the truck starting up. I raced along, running as fast as I could, hoping to reach the spot where I'd get off the road before anybody else could drive by. I was moving so fast I almost overran it. I turned around and waved for the truck. It was almost on top of me. It slowed down and edged off the road onto the little path, rocking over the bumps. I kept motioning for them to come forward. The path didn't go far but it would get them off the road and hopefully out of sight.

"Stop right there," I said, holding up my hands. Any farther and they might not be able to get back out.

The panel truck came to a stop and the two men climbed out.

"Where's your brother, kid?" the little guy asked.

"Not far. He's keeping watch."

"Keeping watch for what?"

"For whatever might get in our way. You're late," I said, trying to change the subject.

"We made a couple of wrong turns. Important thing is we're here," he said.

"Yeah. Grab some branches." I reached down and took a big branch that was lying just beside the path.

Jack and I had cut them earlier. I stood the branch up and leaned it against the back of the vehicle. The two men started to do the same. Branch after branch piled up until the back end was hidden from view, even though I stood only a couple of feet from it.

"You got the raft?" I asked.

"In the truck."

"Get it out and we'd better get going … you're late."

"You mentioned that, kid."

"Yeah, but we have this thing timed and we only have so much light and—"

"Look, kid, you're not my mother or my wife so just stop with the attitude, okay?"

I guessed that even scum like him had a mother. "Sure … yeah … but you were supposed to dress like you were going fishing."

"Oh, yeah, that's right." He unbuttoned his coat, as did the big guy. Underneath their expensive overcoats they were dressed in flannel shirts and dungarees. They took off their coats, folded them and carefully placed them on the front seat. Next they removed their fedoras and placed them on top of their coats. It looked like they had more respect for their clothes than they did for people.

"Is that better?" he asked.

"Much. Come on."

The big guy opened the doors at the side of the van and took hold of a large, inflated rubber raft. As he pulled it out I peered inside the vehicle—there was nobody else there. The second man grabbed four fishing rods and a bright-red tackle box.

"Now we just look like four guys going fishing … if we had the fourth guy. Where's your brother?" This time there was a serious tone in his voice and a threatening look in his eyes.

"We're going to him right now. Just stay here for a second."

I walked up the slope of the path and stopped just before the shelter of the bushes ended. I edged forward and looked up and then down the road. I couldn't see anything, but I knew Jack could see me. I gave him the signal—thumbs up—to let him know everything was okay.

I turned back around. "It's clear!" I yelled. "Come on!"

The two men came waddling along, the raft bouncing up and down between them, the fishing rods peeking over the edge. I scanned the road again. It was still empty.

Up ahead Jack came out of the trees and I quickly joined him.

"Nobody else in the van," I said quietly. "Did you see anything else?"

"Nothing. I think it's just the four of us."

The two men came up beside us. They were both panting and puffing and looked red in the face. This was probably the most physical work they'd done in a while. Maybe that was a good thing—maybe it wasn't. I guessed it depended on whether we were all running from somebody or Jack and I were running from them.

"Come through this way," Jack said.

He brought us down the little path that led to a small, flat clearing right beside the creek. That was the spot where we'd sunned ourselves back in the summer before we'd gone into the creek with our inner tubes. Hard to believe that so much had happened to us in just a few months.

Jack stopped and the two men put the raft down on the sand.

"So far so good," Jack said. "I was just wondering, what do we call you guys?"

"You don't need to know our names," the little guy—who now seemed to be the one in charge—said.

"We need to call you something," Jack explained. "We have to work like a team, and we can't do that if we don't even know your names. What if we need to call out to you to get your attention? Are we supposed to just yell, 'Hey you'?"

The little guy shrugged. "You can call me Red."

What little hair he had certainly didn't look very red.

"It's from when I was a kid and I used to have red hair," he explained.

"And your friend?"

"This is Moose. Say hello, Moose."

"Hello," he said, in a deep baritone voice that matched his size. He reached out and took my hand and shook it. My hand just disappeared in that mighty mitt of his. Despite how big he was, his grip was gentle. He did the same with Jack.

"Before we get started I want to set up some ground rules," Jack said.

"What sort of rules?" Red asked.

"First off, when we're in the camp, *I'm* in charge. I'm the one who knows where things are and how we have to work, so you have to listen to what I say."

Red shrugged his shoulders. "Sure, whatever, kid, as long as you get us the gold. But I want you to understand *my* rules." He reached into his pocket and pulled out his pistol. "My rules are simple. You make a wrong move, either of you," he said, looking at me, "and I put a bullet between your eyes. Kids or no kids, I won't hesitate."

"You don't need to threaten them," Moose said.

"They need to know where things stand," Red said.

"Don't worry, we'll get the gold," Jack said. He sounded confident. He was a good actor. "The second thing is your guns. Are you *both* carrying a gat?"

The two men smiled at each other. Moose patted his shirt to reveal a lump that could only be a gun.

"Never go anywhere without one," Moose said. "Feel like I was half naked if I didn't have it with me."

"You have to give me your word that you won't use them," Jack said, "that you won't shoot any of the guards."

"Last thing in the world we want to do is shoot somebody, including one of you two," Red said. "We're thieves, not killers. We're carrying pieces so we can defend ourselves if we need to, or take prisoners if we have to. We don't want to hurt nobody."

"Good. Then let's stop talking and get into the boat."

CHAPTER NINE

THE RAFT DRIFTED DOWN THE CREEK, lazily spinning and turning as it worked its way through the eddies of water. Jack and I were both paddling but we were making very slow progress.

"We're stuck again," Jack said as the raft pivoted on a low spot. The raft itself was big and it was carrying a pretty heavy load—four bodies ... actually, more like six if you counted how big Moose was.

Without saying a word Jack climbed over the edge of the raft and into the water. I did the same. With the load lightened, and us kicking and pushing, the raft started moving again. Moose reached down then and grabbed me by the arm, effortlessly pulling me up and out of the water and dropping me into the raft beside him. He smiled. I smiled back. It was amazing just how strong he was. He was strong like, like, I guess a moose would be. Jack climbed in over the other side by himself.

"I thought you said this was a good way in to the camp," Red said.

"It's the *best* way. It's just that the water level is

lower than it was the last time we did this, and we weren't carrying this much weight."

"If you want, I can get out and walk," Red suggested. He seemed more than a little anxious.

"No, that wouldn't work. Just sit back and relax," Jack told him.

"Sit back I can do. Relax I can't. I hate boats."

"That's 'cause he can't swim," Moose said.

"I can swim!" Red exclaimed. "Maybe not like some fish but I can do a little doggy-paddle if I need to. Besides, we're in the raft, not in the water."

I looked over at Jack. We were both thinking the same thing—he was going to be in the water before this was over. I just hoped that the pool at the bottom of the waterfall would still be deep enough to catch us, but not deep enough to drown him.

As we rounded another corner in the creek I caught sight of the railroad trestle. Just upstream from it was the large willow that had sheltered Jack and me before. It was right at the edge of the creek and its branches reached over and then down, extending right into the water. Without saying a word we both began paddling to position the raft to enter underneath the overhanging branches. Sluggishly the raft spun slightly around and then over to the right bank. The front end disappeared beneath the branches and we followed. Jack stood up slightly and grabbed a handful of the thin branches, using them as an anchor to stop us from drifting any farther.

"Why are we stopping?" Red asked.

"You see that trestle up there?" Jack asked.

Red turned around and peered through the willow branches.

"We have to wait here for a minute and make sure there isn't a guard coming along there. That's the very farthest corner of the camp. From that point on we're *in* Camp X."

Both Red and Moose looked up at the trestle. I turned around so I could see back up the creek, the way we'd come. If something was following and it wanted to be close enough to keep up with us, it would have to appear pretty soon.

"If we do see a guard when we're going under the trestle we have to pretend we're fishing," Jack said. "We'll paddle. You two should get your fishing rods out and put a line in the water."

"Yeah, yeah, good plan," Red said.

They began fiddling with the rods. Jack and I didn't do much fishing, but it was obvious that these guys had *never* been fishing before. They fumbled with the reels and hardly seemed to know which end of the rod to hold.

Red peered through the overhanging branches and up at the bridge. "I don't see nobody."

"Me neither," Moose said, although he wasn't even looking in the right direction.

"Good, then we're safe to go." Jack let loose his grip on the branches and the raft began drifting. It bumped into the shore and Jack used his paddle to push off and out. The raft started to spin sideways and I paddled frantically to correct it. It would be bad enough going over the falls as it was—I didn't even want to *think* about going over backwards.

We cleared the overhanging branches and were aimed right at the middle of the creek. That was good because, ideally, we wanted to pass through the middle span of the trestle. Jack and I paddled while Red and Moose pretended to fish. Their lines were in the water but they didn't have bait—or even hooks, for that matter. That was probably good. I didn't think either of them would know what to do with a live fish. Maybe Red would threaten to shoot it and Moose would eat it raw and whole!

The side of the raft brushed against one of the cement foundations of the bridge but it slipped through. I looked up at the wooden crossbeams and then at the tracks directly above my head. I couldn't help thinking about standing up there, earlier in the day, looking down, and then the train coming right toward me. If I had still been on that bridge it would have been all over right there. This could have ended before it had barely even started.

I also thought about the very first time I'd ever seen the bridge. Jack and I had been drifting in our old inner tubes, cooling off, hidden beneath the branches of that willow. We'd looked up in surprise, confusion and then shock as we saw what we thought were enemy agents planting explosives, trying to blow it up. We'd later found out that the "explosives" were just lumps of clay and the "enemy agents" were guys being trained at Camp X to be spies.

If we hadn't seen them that day we never would have gone into the camp to investigate. And if we hadn't done that, then everything that followed—including this—wouldn't have happened either. Instead of being here, drifting along the river with two armed criminals trying to break into a spy camp to steal gold, we'd be sitting in school, dreaming about doing something more interesting than studying. Sometimes it's best that you don't get what you wish for.

I was startled out of my thoughts when I was hit by a splattering of water. I looked up and over at Jack. He'd splashed me with his paddle, and now he was gesturing with his head for me to look back. There was a long stretch of creek but I didn't see anything— that was what he was showing me. Sure, that had to be it. We were alone, and nobody was following us.

"Stay awake," he mouthed at me.

That was good advice. Now that we were past the trestle we were headed toward the drop. The first time we'd gone over—which as far as I was concerned at the time was going to be the *only* time I ever went over—it was a complete surprise. We'd been drifting down the stream, enjoying the sun and the cool of the water, and then *whoosh*! Five or ten seconds of terror and then it was over, practically before I'd figured out what was going on.

Now I knew what was going to happen. I knew it was coming. It was around the next curve or the next or the next. And even more troubling was what was going to happen after the falls. What would these two men—these two armed criminals—say to us? Would they be mad and blame us? What were they going to do to us? This was going to be so much worse than the first time.

The current seemed to be picking up speed. I looked over at Jack. He'd noticed it too, but thank goodness he was the only other one who had. The two men just sat there, clueless. Red did look anxious, but that was just his nervousness around the boat and water. If he'd had any idea what was going to play out he would have been a lot more than anxious.

The banks of the creek rose on both sides and the increase in the current and our speed was really noticeable. We were getting close. Now there was nothing we could do even if we wanted to. We were going over the falls.

The raft started to ripple as it rolled over little drops along the way, and it felt like it was alive and trying to buck us right out. I dropped the paddle to the bottom of the raft. Paddling was pointless. Steering was useless. The creek was now in complete control. I grabbed onto the lip of the raft with both hands and dug my fingers in as deeply as I could. ·

Red turned around to face us. His expression had gone from anxious to scared.

"What's happening?" he yelled over the rush of the water.

"Hold on!" Jack yelled back.

Red's eyes widened in panic. "What are you—? AAAAHHHHH!"

The front end of the raft—and Red and Moose—disappeared over the drop. I held both my breath and the lip of the raft, hanging on for dear life, and then I found myself flying through the air, head first, arms extended in front of me. Was this how Superman felt? Before I could think of an answer, I got an answer. I hit the water, somersaulting over and then shooting beneath the surface!

CHAPTER TEN

INSTINCTIVELY I'D CLOSED MY MOUTH and my eyes as we flew through the air and smashed into the water. Now I kept my mouth closed but opened my eyes. Looking up, I could see daylight streaming down through the waving, bubbling water. I tried to claw my way to the surface but it felt like I was moving in slow motion. Actually, I wasn't moving at all! I was suspended, struggling to claw my way to the top while my feet were being pulled to the bottom. I kicked my feet to try to break free, wishing I weren't wearing shoes or heavy, soaked clothing. I couldn't seem to move. Strange … I didn't feel panicky … I felt calm, almost safe, protected and sheltered and hidden beneath the water.

Suddenly, somehow, I surged upward and shot out of the water. I gasped in a big breath of air. Before I could see anything I heard yelling. I turned around. It was Red. He was screaming and splashing and thrashing around in the water, and then he just disappeared beneath the surface!

Jack and Moose swam toward where he'd been. Jack dove down, his shoes the last thing visible. I treaded water, watching, waiting. Red broke to the surface, along with Jack, my brother's arm around his neck. He was struggling wildly, trying to break free, and now that he could get air into his lungs he started to scream again! He was swinging his arms around like a wild man, thrashing in the water and hitting Jack! Moose reached over and slugged Red. His fist just plowed into Red's jaw! Red stopped struggling. He slumped over, and then Moose grabbed onto him. Together he and Jack started to tow Red to shore.

"The raft!" Jack called out to me. "Get the raft!"

I looked around. It was upside down and drifting downstream. I stopped treading water and swam toward it. The current wasn't very strong and I quickly caught up. I grabbed onto the side. For a split second I thought about trying to right it but I knew that wouldn't be possible. Instead I held on with one hand and did a side stroke with the other to haul it back to shore. I had to drag it along until the water was shallow enough to put my feet down. I stood up then and started to tow it.

Jack and Moose had carried Red over to a small sand patch on the bank of the creek. He was lying on his back and the two of them were bent over him. He wasn't moving. Oh my goodness, he wasn't moving! Then suddenly Red sat up and began coughing violently, and he spat up water, an unbelievable amount of water. Had he swallowed half the creek?

I beached the raft on the sandbar and went over and squatted beside them.

"Red, can you hear me? Say something!" Moose demanded.

He didn't answer.

"Are you okay?" Jack asked.

Red reached out and grabbed Jack by the throat, pulling him down toward him as he pulled himself up. Then, almost like magic, his gun was in his hand and he was holding it to the side of Jack's head! What was he doing?

"You tried to kill me!" he screamed. "I should blow your brains out, you stinking little—"

"He didn't try to kill nobody," Moose said.

"He took us over the waterfall!" Red was still in a fury. "He knew it was there and he thought he could drown us!"

He lowered the gun as he looked over at Moose.

Like lightning Moose reached out and smacked the gun away with one hand, broke Red's grip on Jack with the other and then dropped his full weight on Red's chest! I couldn't believe that anybody that big could possibly move that fast!

"What do you think you're—?"

"Shut up!" Moose hissed. "Shut up and stop yelling. You want to let every guard from everywhere around know that we're here?"

Red didn't answer—with Moose's weight on his chest I didn't think Red *could* have answered.

"I'm letting you up," Moose said quietly, "but don't you go doing any more yelling, you understand?"

Red, who was actually turning red in the face, nodded, and Moose shifted off of him. Slowly Red sat up.

"You tried to kill me," he said to Jack. He turned to me. "Both of you tried to kill me." A chill went up my spine.

"We didn't try to kill you, honestly!"

"You've been down this way before. You knew there was a waterfall."

"We knew, but we didn't know it was here," I lied. "We thought it was farther down … we didn't know. We just weren't thinking right because we were scared, that's all."

"I don't believe you," he hissed.

"You think they'd have put themselves over a waterfall if they'd known?" Moose asked.

That was a good point. Who would do something that stupid … other than Jack and me?

"Look, Red, that kid saved your life," Moose said. "He was the one that got you when you went under, and do you think I could have dragged you out of the water without him?"

Red didn't answer.

"If anything, the kid should be mad at *you*," Moose

continued. "Look at what you did to his face."

I looked over at Jack. I hadn't noticed but there were four, bright-red, angry-looking scratches on his cheek!

"When you was struggling you reached back and raked him with your nails. Kid's lucky you didn't take out an eye. That's why I had to slug you," Moose said. "You mad at me for that?"

Red sort of shook his head.

"'Sides, even if you are mad at the kid—and I don't think he did anything wrong—you still gotta know that if you do anything to him, anything that stops us from getting the gold, then you might as well be putting that gun to your own head and pulling the trigger."

What did he mean by that?

"Just think about what Dom would do to you if you screwed this up," Moose went on.

Dom … that had to be the boss guy. That was his name, Dom.

Red nodded his head slowly in response.

Moose reached over, picked Red's gun up off the sand and handed it to him. Seemed to me that wasn't the smartest thing to do. Red held the gun in his hand. He looked at Jack and then at me. I held my breath. He tucked the gun back into his pocket. Moose reached down and helped him to his feet.

"You ready to go?" Moose asked.

"I'm okay ... I guess ... but where's the tackle box?"

"The what?"

"The tackle box, the red tackle box."

"It must have fallen out of the raft when we went over the—"

"There it is!" Jack said, pointing to the far side of the pool. The bright-red tackle box was bobbing along. "I'll get it."

Jack waded into the water and then dove forward. He did the crawl, quickly closed the distance and reached the box. Rather than grabbing it, he made a turn and then pushed it back in front of him, tapping it forward with one hand and then taking a stroke to catch up to it. He looked sort of like a trained seal playing with a ball. When he got closer, Moose waded into the water and picked it up.

"That was lucky," Moose said.

"It's not like we're really going fishing or anything," I pointed out.

Moose laughed—a deep, low chuckle. "I guess in some ways we are."

He undid the two latches and popped open the tackle box.

"All snug and dry," Moose said. "The box must be waterproof."

"What's in there?" I asked, trying to peer around him.

"Stuff we'll be needing when we get closer." He closed the lid and did the buckles back up. "So, where do we go now?"

"We have to go farther downstream, so I guess back into the boat," Jack said.

"No way." Red held up his arms like he was surrendering. "There's no way I'm getting back in another boat for the rest of my life."

"It's the only way we can get there," Jack said.

"I'll walk along beside the creek."

"You can't do that. We're heading into a marsh so there's no place to walk."

"It'll be okay," I said reassuringly. "We're past the waterfall, and there's only one of them on the creek."

"Are you sure?" Red asked. He sounded like he didn't believe me. I couldn't blame him.

"Honest, for sure," I said. "We were wrong about where it was but we aren't wrong about how many there are. Just one. The current is even pretty weak here because the creek is so much wider."

He didn't say yes, but he didn't say no. Slowly he rose to his feet. He looked unsteady, shaky, as he walked over to the raft. He grabbed it and flipped it over so it was sitting the right way, then he touched the side with his hand, like he was checking to see if it was still solid and sound. He turned around.

"Okay, let's go."

Red climbed right into the raft, right in the middle,

and braced himself so his arms and legs were outstretched and stuck into the rubber sides. Jack and Moose and I all pushed it off the sandbar and into the water. Moose waded in, then jumped in, and the whole thing buckled under his weight. For a split second I thought it was going to flip over, sending Red into the drink again. Red let out a little squeal, so I guess he thought the same thing. The raft settled down and I jumped in.

Jack kept pushing and then held on but didn't climb in. He floated behind the raft instead, kicking his legs to power it forward.

"It's not much farther now," I said to the two men, trying to make conversation.

"Can't be too soon for me," Red muttered.

"I'm just happy that nobody has seen us," I said.

"Or heard us," Moose added to Red. "You were screaming like a little girl."

"I was drowning. What did you expect me to sound like?"

Moose shrugged. "Not like a little girl drowning."

I had to fight the urge to laugh. I didn't think Red liked Moose poking fun at him, but there was nothing much he could do about it. He could probably do a lot of things about me laughing at him, though, so I'd avoid doing that.

The banks of the creek had been replaced now by rows and rows of tall bulrushes. Riding low in the water we were hidden from view. Jack stopped kicking and waded alongside the boat.

"You can get out and help if you want," he said to me.

"You stay put," Moose told me. "I'll take care of it." He crawled over to the edge of the raft, and the shift in weight sent the far side up into the air, threatening to tip it over again. Red scrambled to try to balance the boat and Moose flopped over the side and into the water, causing the raft to buck like a wild bronco before settling back down. I couldn't help but wonder if Moose was just being clumsy because he was so big or whether he'd done it deliberately to bother Red. I climbed out as well, leaving Red on his own, once again straddling the centre of the raft. I wondered if he'd stay firmly lodged there until it had been dragged up onto dry land.

I waded along beside the raft. Moose and Jack didn't need my help to tow. The water got shallower with each step until we reached a little lip of muddy shore. As I climbed up onto the land I was startled by two red-winged blackbirds that flew out of the reeds, noisily screaming as they soared into the sky. I guess I'd startled them too. I had the urge to yell at them to be quiet—like that made any sense.

We were surrounded on all sides by the bulrushes. They were tall enough to not only block our view, but also to prevent anybody from seeing us.

"We have to hide the raft," Jack said.

"Looks pretty well hidden right now," Red answered.

"Not from all directions," Jack said, pointing up to the sky.

Red snorted. "Like a plane is going to see it."

"Planes take off and land here all the time," I said. "If they saw an abandoned raft they'd radio down and have somebody come and investigate."

Red didn't look happy with my answer. I guessed he didn't like being told he was wrong.

Jack snapped the stalk of a bulrush. He wiggled it back and forth until it broke off. "We can cover it with these so it blends in."

"That would pretty well take forever," Red said.

"We've got time. We're not going anywhere until it gets dark. Besides, it won't take that long if all four of us work together."

"It won't be four," Red said. He sat down.

Jack looked like he was going to say something, but he didn't. Instead he turned away and walked over to a thick patch of bulrushes and began bending one back to break it off. I went over as well and started to do the same.

"Here, this'll help," Moose said.

I turned around. He was holding some sort of handle. How would that help?

He flicked a little switch and a six-inch blade flipped out! The blade glistened in the light. He offered it, handle first, to Jack.

"Be careful, it's real sharp," he said.

"Maybe you should use it," Jack suggested.

"Naw. I'll use this one instead." With his other hand he reached down and pulled up one leg of his pants to reveal a knife in a leather sheath strapped to his leg. He pulled it out and held it up. It had to be twice as long as the other knife.

"I figure you and me cut and George brings them back and puts them on the raft," Moose said.

"That would work," Jack agreed. He took the first knife from Moose.

They began cutting. The knives were obviously very sharp and they sliced through the reeds effortlessly. Quickly there was a pile. I gathered up the first few and brought them over to the raft. I placed them against the sides, leaning them over so they covered more of the raft.

Jack was moving in one direction, cutting, and Moose had started off the other way. I scrambled to keep up. This would have been easier if Red had been helping as well. Instead he just sat there, watching out of the corner of his eye. I wasn't sure if he was being lazy or just didn't like being ordered around by a kid. Either way, we were getting the job done without him.

"How's it coming along?" Jack asked as I came back over to where he was piling up reeds.

"Fine. Fast. Almost a quarter of it is covered

already," I said. "It won't take long. By the way, that was pretty scary back there."

"It was just a little dip in the water, nothing to be scared of."

"I didn't mean that part," I said, although that was pretty scary. "I meant Red holding that gun to your head."

"Hardly had time to get scared before Moose jumped him," Jack said. "Besides, it wasn't like he could have actually shot me."

"I don't know," I said. "I figure he's the sort of guy who might shoot somebody."

"You're probably right. That is, if he had a gun that worked."

"Why would you think his gun wouldn't work?" I asked.

"It was under water, remember?"

"Oh, yeah, that's right! So it wouldn't have been able to fire."

"Good thing," Jack said, "because I think you're right. Red wouldn't think twice about putting a pill into somebody."

"I'm just glad Moose was there. He wouldn't let him hurt us—he's different," I said.

"Different, yes, but that doesn't mean better," Jack said. "Maybe he wouldn't use a gun, but I'd bet he'd snap your head off if you got in his way. Either way you'd be just as dead."

"I don't know," I said.

"Think about it," Jack said. "He didn't have any problem smacking his friend, did he?"

"I guess not, but he did stop Red from hurting you."

"He stopped him because he knows they can't kill us." He handed me an armful of bulrushes. "At least, they can't kill us yet."

I really didn't like the sound of that. Jack came closer.

"Until we get the gold," he said, his voice just a whisper, "we're safe."

"And after?"

"After may be different. I don't think these guys are really going to count on us to take our gold bar and keep our mouths shut. I think maybe they're just stringing us along until they get what they want, and after that they're planning to shut us up … permanently. But I think I have that figured out."

"What are you two whispering about?" Red asked. He was standing just behind us.

"We're just trying to keep our voices down," Jack said. "We're all lucky nobody heard you screaming like a little girl when you went into the water."

Red snarled.

What was Jack doing? Did he think it was smart to taunt the guy with the gun?

"I think I screamed too," I said, trying to defuse the situation. "Do you think you could carry these back?" I asked, holding out the reeds.

"Carry 'em yourself," Red said, and he turned and walked away.

I waited until he was clearly out of earshot. "So what's your idea?"

"After we get the gold and get back into the raft, you're going to have to get away," Jack said.

"Get away?"

"You're going to slip away, maybe into the water, and just vanish."

"Shouldn't both of us get away?" I asked.

Jack shook his head. "If we both get away they'll kill Mom. I'm going to go with them and deliver the gold and get Mom. You're going to go back to where we camped."

"And do what?"

"Nothing. You just wait. If we're okay, we'll come and get you."

"And if you don't come?"

"Then you go right back into Camp X. Find Bill. Tell him everything, and we'll hope it isn't too late."

"Too late for what?" I asked.

"Too late for us to be saved."

"Don't talk like that. I'm sure it'll all work out."

"Maybe, but we have to make …" Jack swivelled his head. "Do you hear something?"

I listened. Yeah, there was something … the sound of an engine. Was it a car, or jeep or—?

"Everybody get in the reeds!" Jack yelled out.

Before I could even think to react Jack grabbed my hand and yanked me forward. He dove headfirst into the bulrushes and I jumped in after him, landing almost on top of him.

"It's a plane!" Jack said.

I looked through the reeds and up into the sky. I could hear the engine—it was getting louder—but I couldn't see anything in the sky. No, there it was! A small, single-engine plane zipped by! It was black, no markings whatsoever, and it cut across the sky, just over from us. It was gone in a few seconds, and the noise of the engine faded away.

"Do you think it saw us?" I asked.

"Doubt it. If it had it would have most likely doubled back for a better look. I think we're safe."

"Maybe now Red won't argue so much the next time we tell him we have to do something," I suggested.

"I doubt it. Let's keep moving."

CHAPTER ELEVEN

"HOW MUCH LONGER before we go?" I asked Jack.

"Soon."

The sun had been down below the horizon for about fifteen minutes but there was light spilling over the edge. My clothes were still damp and I was feeling cold. We were safe where we were, hidden at the edge of the marsh, but we'd have to wait for complete darkness before we attempted to break free and cross the more open section of field leading to the catacombs.

"You boys have done well to get us this far," Moose said.

He sounded like a teacher congratulating us on doing well on a test. I had to remember that he wasn't a teacher and that Jack was probably right—he'd kill us too.

"The catacombs are over there," Jack said to Red, pointing the way across the field in the gathering darkness.

"Just up from the cliffs," Red agreed. "Maybe we should go that way, down by the water, and then climb up the cliff."

"I thought you'd probably want to avoid the water," Jack said, and then he chuckled softly to himself.

Why was he taunting Red again? That was so typical of Jack—if someone was pushing him around, he just had to push right back, whatever way he could.

"The cliff is too steep to climb," I explained. "Especially at night."

"Besides, they have lots of guards on the perimeter of the camp, lots of eyes looking for people to come in off the lake. We'd be seen for sure if we tried to come in that way. Here, we're already inside the camp, and nobody is looking in this direction. The guards are all looking *out,* not *in.*"

"You boys know what you're doing," Moose said, before Red could comment. "So how do we get there from here?"

"We follow that line of trees," Jack said, pointing across the field. "It'll lead us close. Do you know how many guards there are at the catacombs once we get there?"

"Two outside and two inside is what we were told."

"Then they outnumber you two," I said.

"Even numbers. We're gonna take 'em two at a time, and we have the element of surprise," Red said.

"And I'm probably bigger than all four of them put together," Moose said.

"But these guys have special training," I pointed out. "They know how to defend themselves."

Moose chuckled. "I'm not so worried. Before we go I better give you boys something." He grabbed the tackle box that was by his side. I'd been more than a little curious about what he had in there. He opened it.

"Here, take one of these."

He handed me a hat, a black hat. I was cold, but why would he have brought hats?

"When we get close to the catacombs, pull it down over your face," Moose said.

"But how will I see?"

"Through the eyeholes. It's a balaclava."

"I've heard of those," Jack said. "Skiers use them sometimes."

"That's the ticket. They want their faces protected from the cold. We want our faces protected from being identified. To take the guards out we have to be practically in their faces, and we don't want them to be able to finger us later on. No use in stealing the gold if we can't stay out of jail and enjoy it."

"But we're not going to hurt them, right?" I asked.

"What we're gonna have to do maybe will hurt them, but it isn't gonna kill them," Moose said.

"If we were going to waste them we wouldn't be worrying none about hiding our faces," Red said. "Dead people can't identify you in a lineup. We want everybody to walk away."

He was right, and that was reassuring ... until I remembered that Jack and I had seen everybody's faces, his and Moose's and even Dom's. More and more I was thinking they weren't going to let us walk away.

Moose handed everybody a balaclava and we put them on the tops of our heads.

"What else you got in that box?" Jack asked.

"Some lengths of rope, handcuffs and tape."

"Why do you have tape?" I asked.

"Same reason we have the rope and handcuffs. We're gonna have to make sure these guys aren't going anywhere."

"But how will tape stop them?"

"It stops them from yelling," Red said. "We tape their mouths shut so they can't call for help."

"If all goes well, then nothing will be discovered until the change in guards tomorrow morning, and by then we'll be long gone," Moose explained.

"Yeah, us and some of the gold."

"How much of the gold are we going to take?" Jack asked.

"As much as we can carry back to the van," Red said.

"And how much is that?" Jack questioned.

"There's going to be more gold there than four people can carry. There's probably enough gold it'd take a hundred guys to cart it away!"

"Seriously?" I asked.

"Seriously. The entire gold reserves of the Bank of England. We're not talking millions of dollars, we're talking a *billion* dollars."

"I can't even imagine how much gold that would be," I said.

"It's a mountain. We're just taking a few straws from the haystack and leaving a fortune behind," Red said.

"But we're still taking a small fortune with us just the same," Moose said. "The gold comes in bars, and each bar weighs twenty-five pounds."

"That's heavy," I said. "I know I can carry two bars ... maybe three."

"You'll take three," Red said. That wasn't a suggestion—that was an order.

"I can carry four," Jack said.

"And I'm good for five or six," Red added.

Six bars would be one hundred and fifty pounds. Red was stocky and strong-looking but he couldn't have weighed much more than that.

"And Moose here, he's good for at least six bars, maybe seven," Red said.

"Maybe eight," Moose bragged.

"I don't know," I said. "The truck is a long way from here and it's uphill and it's going to be dark and we have to travel through the woods and—"

"Let's just get it back to the raft and we'll tow it most of the way," Red said.

"What about the waterfall?"

"We'll carry it around that. It won't be quick, but we should have six hours before anybody notices what happened—plenty of time."

"I guess so. So how much is twenty bars of gold worth?" I asked.

"A fortune," Red said.

"And we get to keep one bar, right?" I asked.

Moose smiled. "One bar."

"And you two split the rest between you," I said.

"We get a cut of the rest," Red said. "You know, we have to share with our associate."

"You mean your boss?" Jack asked.

"Our partner."

"Partner? Seems like he does all the talking while you two take all the risks and do all the work."

"It was his idea, and he came up with the plan," Red said, defending him.

"So he's the brains and you two are the muscle," Jack said. "I guess he doesn't get as big a share as you two."

Neither man answered. That meant he was getting at least as much as them.

"It's dark enough," Red said. "Let's get moving."

Slowly Jack rose to his feet, and we all did the same. We had been hidden behind the reeds but now we were peeking over the top. We were looking out at an open field—a field that we had to cross to get to the protection of the line of trees. It was quiet and dark. Twice while we'd been waiting we'd heard jeeps being driven, and once we'd seen a patrol as it crossed through the field on the far side. We could only hope that nothing would come while we were crossing. If it did, we'd have to drop to the ground and stay motionless and silent and hope it would pass by without seeing us.

Jack led the way, followed by Red, then me, then Moose. Although Jack was only a half-dozen paces ahead he was almost invisible. He looked more like a darker shade of black against the night. Above our heads the sky was cloudless and a million stars sparkled. There was a quarter moon and it was shining down on us brightly. I was grateful for the light to help us see but afraid of being seen because of it.

In the distance I heard the roar of an engine and I startled. Everybody stopped dead in their tracks and listened. It was getting louder. Then we saw two little headlights bobbing along in the distance. A jeep was crossing the field we'd just crossed, and it was coming in our direction!

"Get into the trees!" Jack hissed.

Quickly we all took shelter within the thin line of trees. If it had been day we'd have been clearly visible but in the darkness we had a good shot at staying hidden. The jeep continued to move slowly. It looked like it was almost following the route we'd travelled, right along the trees.

"As long as we stay here, stay quiet and don't move we'll be okay," Jack said.

"I got a better idea," Moose said. "You two stay low, and, Red, you cover me when I need it."

What was he talking about? What was he going to do? I stayed low to the ground, pressed up against Jack. Neither Red nor Moose moved either.

The jeep got closer and closer. I tried to look behind the bright lights to see how many guys were in it. I could make out the shadow of a driver and maybe a second person. As it came closer the headlights swept over us, but the driver wasn't looking into the trees. The jeep was right beside us and it kept moving—it hadn't seen us. Then Moose stood up and ran toward the jeep! He leaped up and into the back of it! The engine roared and then the jeep swerved, hitting one of the trees with a thud. The noise of the engine stopped and the lights died, leaving everything in total darkness. Red ran out, gun in hand. Jack and I stayed where we were, frozen in place.

"Cover your face," Jack hissed, and I pulled the balaclava over my face as he did the same.

We ran over to the jeep. Moose and Red, holding their pistols, stood over two soldiers, who were huddled on the ground.

"Get the box," Red ordered.

For a split second I didn't move because I didn't realize what he was talking about, or that it was me he was talking to.

"Get moving!" he barked, and I sprang to life, running back to where we'd been hidden in the trees. I didn't see the tackle box right away and I had to feel around until I found it lying on its side in the tall grass. I brought it over.

The two soldiers were now on their feet, leaning with their hands against the side of the jeep.

"Both of you, take off your uniforms," Red ordered.

"What?" one of them asked in disbelief. I thought I recognized his voice.

Red put his gun to the soldier's head. "You think I'm joking around here?"

The two soldiers began taking off their coats and shirts. It wasn't long before they were standing there in their undershirts and shorts.

Moose took the tackle box from me. He opened it and removed a piece of rope. He used it to tie the hands of one of the soldiers together. He then did the same with the second. Next he bound their legs, and then he took the tape and sealed off their mouths. Moose picked one of them up—it was like he wasn't even straining—and put him down among the trees. He then did the same with the second.

"You know how to drive one of these things?" Red asked Jack.

"Sure."

"Good. You're gonna drive. But first you boys better get into the uniforms."

"What?" I must have sounded even more shocked than the soldier did when Moose asked him to get *out* of the uniform.

"Get into the uniforms. I got a plan. A plan that will let us get away with a whole lot more of the gold than I thought we could."

CHAPTER TWELVE

JACK SLOWLY BUMPED the jeep across the field. I sat at his side in a uniform that was way too big. I felt like I was swimming in it rather than wearing it, but at least it was dry. Like every other kid in the country I'd thought about what it would be like to someday wear my country's uniform, but this certainly wasn't the way I'd dreamed about it.

I rolled back the sleeves so my hands were free. If it hadn't been for the fact that I was sitting in the jeep, partially hidden, there was no way I would have fooled anybody. Jack looked a bit more believable, though, because he filled out the uniform. As for me, I looked like I was wearing my father's clothes. And what would our father think about what we were wearing, what we were doing? He was in uniform to defend our country. We were wearing uniforms to *steal* from our country. We were so proud of him, and if he'd known what we were doing he would have been so ashamed of us. *I* was ashamed of us. I just wished we had a choice.

"It's up ahead," Jack said. He brought the jeep to a stop.

"Do you think they're in position?" I asked. Red and Moose had left on foot ten minutes ahead of us so they could circle around the entrance to the catacombs to come at them from the rear.

"Maybe. Let's just wait another couple of minutes to be sure. If we arrive before them then it's over. We'll be captured wearing these uniforms. That would make us spies. And you know what they do with spies."

"The same thing they do with people who break the Official Secrets Act. Either way, we're—"

"I know," Jack said, "I know. Now, this may be the only time we're going to be alone, so this is the last chance I might have to tell you what you need to do. Listen and listen good."

"I'm listening."

"Like I said before, as soon as we get out of the camp with the gold you have to slip away. Once Red and Moose notice that you're gone they're going to try to find you, maybe yell that if you don't come out they're going to kill me. No matter what they say you keep going. If you come back, then I'm dead. We're all dead. The only chance we have is for you to get free. And remember, if Mom and I don't show up, then you go to the authorities."

"And what am I going to tell them?"

"Everything you know. Tell them about the gold and about Red and Moose and how their boss is named Dom. The police must know these guys. Okay?"

"I'm okay," I said, "but I feel like I'm melting."

"I'm sweating up a storm too," Jack said.

We had slipped on the uniforms over our clothes, and of course our faces and heads were covered by the balaclavas.

"Now it's time." Jack put the jeep into gear and flicked on the headlights. The dirt track in front of us was lit as we slowly bumped along. We came to a crossroads. Directly ahead was the main part of the camp—the barracks and the classrooms and the shooting range and headquarters. Bill would probably be asleep, but he might be there sitting at his desk working on something. And even if he wasn't, they'd get him up pretty fast if we appeared at the front door.

"Jack, I have another idea."

"You do?"

"What if we drove up to the main building and found Bill directly and told him what was happening, and he got his men and they captured Red and Moose right now and—"

"Sure, and then their contact inside the camp might hear what happened and tell Dom. Or Red and Moose might get away. And even if nothing went wrong, we still wouldn't know where Mom is being held captive. Face it, we have no choice."

Jack turned right, toward the cliff, the shore and the catacombs.

The road was a lot smoother than I remembered it. Before, it used to be nothing more than a path leading down to the cliff. Now it was a real gravel road. That made sense. Before, the catacombs were just some empty caves. Now, they held a fortune in gold.

"Remember, let me do all the talking," Jack said. "If they hear your little boy voice they'll know you're not a soldier."

Jack was driving in first gear, going only a few miles an hour. We didn't know the road and we didn't exactly know where the entrance to the catacombs was. Besides, we had to make sure to leave time for Red and Moose to get into position.

"Up ahead," I said. "Do you see it?"

"I don't see … wait a second … a little red glowing light. Somebody is smoking."

"It has to be one of the guards."

The light vanished for a split second, then reappeared and rose. We could see the outline of a rocky outcrop. The jeep went forward and in the sweep of the headlights two guards appeared, rifles on their soldiers, one with a cigarette in his hand. They held up their hands to shield their eyes from the headlights.

Jack brought the jeep to a stop, then stood up in his seat and leaned against the windshield.

"How's it going?" he yelled out, disguising his voice to make it deeper and older-sounding.

"Was going fine until somebody aimed his headlights at us!" one of the guards called back. "Turn 'em off, you're practically blinding us!"

That was the idea.

Before Jack could answer, two figures came flying out of the darkness and into the light! Moose bashed into the man who had spoken and sent him crashing to the ground. Before he could even make a sound Moose had pounced on him, hitting him in the side of the head!

Red simply put a gun to the head of the other man. As he put his hands up in the air Red slipped the man's rifle off his shoulder.

"Turn off the lights!" Red called out, and suddenly the whole scene disappeared into the darkness.

Moose ran over to the jeep, reached into the back and grabbed the tackle box. "Get out of those uniforms and come and help," he said, and then he was gone.

We didn't need a second invitation. Quickly we stripped off the uniforms. I just wished I could take off the balaclava, but I knew I needed that.

We got out of the jeep and stumbled forward in the darkness until we reached Red. The one guard was on his knees in front of him now, his hands on the back of his head and the pistol shoved in his face.

"I'm only gonna ask one more time," Red said ominously. "How many men are inside?"

"Why should I tell you?" the guard said. He was trying to sound brave but his voice was shaking with fear. I couldn't see his face clearly enough in the dark to know whether his expression matched his voice.

"You'll tell me 'cause if you don't you're gonna get real dead. Your buddy over there is all safe and sound—unconscious, but safe and sound. My partner is tying him up. You tell me and we'll tie you up too. In a few hours they'll find him, alive. You don't tell me, and they'll find one of you dead. You want to wake up dead?"

There was no answer, and then I heard the distinctive click of a pistol being cocked, ready to fire!

"You shoot me and there'll be twenty guards on you in seconds," the man said.

"That won't make you any less dead," Red replied.

"And it won't help you get out of here alive with the gold."

Moose came out of the darkness now and walked over to the guard. He reached down and grabbed the man's head and pulled him to his feet. Then he hoisted him up higher and held him up in the air above his head!

"Me snapping your neck won't make a sound," Moose said softly.

"I'll talk … I'll tell." The guard's voice was barely audible.

Moose held him there a few more seconds, laughing—he was enjoying this! Finally he released the man, who dropped to the ground with a thud.

"So how many guards are inside?" Red asked.

"Just one!" the guard said, his voice now raspy and harsh.

"You lying to me?" Red asked. "How come there isn't a second man?"

"There usually are two!" the guard said pleadingly. "But the last few nights there's only been one … honestly. Please believe me!"

"I do believe you. Now what's this one guy's name?"

"It's … it's … James."

"And what do you usually call him?" Red asked.

"What do you mean?"

"Do you call him James or Jimmy or Jim? What name do you call him?"

"Jimbo, I call him Jimbo. Everybody calls him Jimbo."

"Good, then that's the name you're going to use when you call him."

I understood what he was doing.

"Get up and keep your hands where I can see them," Red ordered. "Don't try anything … or else."

Slowly the guard got up. He was still rubbing his head. I backed slightly away. I didn't want him to get a good look at me. Even though I was wearing the balaclava it was obvious that I wasn't very big. Maybe he thought I was a woman.

"You know you're not going to get away with this," the guard said.

"We're doing pretty good so far, don't you think?" Red answered.

"There are guards everywhere."

"Not the way we came in—or the way we're going out. Now, one more question. What's your name?"

"My name?"

"What do people call you?"

"Freddie, mostly Freddie."

"Good, and a final question. When we get into the cave, where will we find good old Jimbo?"

"He'll be toward the back … there's a little desk … that's where he sits … it's not so easy to find."

"It'll be easy for us to find because you're taking us there. Let's go."

Red grabbed the guard and pushed him forward, still holding the gun at his side. Moose motioned for us to follow. We fell into line, Jack behind Moose and me at the end.

Suddenly there was a beam of light and I jumped backwards, startled. It was from a flashlight aimed at the entrance to the catacombs, a large metal door that seemed to be built right into the rock face.

"Use your key to unlock the door," Red said softly. "And no tricks."

I heard keys jangling together before I saw them in the lock. The door swung inward.

"Call out to him. Let him know we're coming," Red said, his voice barely audible.

"Hello!" the guard yelled into the cave. "Jimbo! It's me, Freddie, I'm coming in!"

There was no answer. That couldn't be good.

"Jimbo, you sleeping or what?" the guard called out.

"Not sleeping any more!" a voice echoed out of the darkness.

"Just thought you might want to come up for some air, maybe have a smoke," the guard called back.

"Maybe that wouldn't be such a bad idea," the voice—Jimbo's—answered.

Red shoved the guard in the back with the pistol and the guard stumbled forward. Moose had to duck slightly to get through the doorway. Jack followed. I hesitated at the door for a split second before stepping inside.

Instantly it was cooler and the air was damp. We were in the dark, but ahead of us the light showed the way. The floors were wooden planks, but the walls were just sheer rock—it was a cave. As we walked the space opened up, and the little beam of light couldn't find the wall on the other side.

"Hey, Jimbo!" Freddie called out. His voice sounded shaky. "Maybe you should turn on some lights so we can see you!"

All at once the whole room was bathed in bright light and—

"Drop your weapons!" yelled out a voice, and all around us soldiers appeared.

I started to raise my hands when Moose spun around and began firing his pistol!

CHAPTER THIRTEEN

"PUT YOUR HANDS UP and drop your weapons!" the voice yelled out again.

I started to raise my hands when Moose turned and ran toward the door. There were explosions and flashes of light, and suddenly something smashed into me, sending me flying into the air. When I landed, something huge fell on top of me. It was Moose, and his weight forced the air out of my lungs.

"Cease fire!" a voice shouted, and the gunfire stopped. Everything stopped. I lay there, pinned beneath Moose, unable to move, unable to draw a full breath.

Out of the corner of my eye I saw movement. I twisted my head slightly. There were soldiers—there had to be ten or twelve of them—and they were appearing from all sides of the cave!

"Hands up!" A soldier poked a rifle into my face.

"I can't," I gasped. "I can't move! I'm pinned down!"

I felt the weight lift off my chest as two men pulled Moose off me. He was limp and he wasn't moving, and as they dropped him to the ground beside me I realized there was a gaping hole in his chest and he was bleeding! Then I saw that my shirt was covered with blood, and for a split second I wondered if I'd been shot, until I realized it was Moose's blood.

I was grabbed roughly by the collar and hoisted to my feet. What about Jack? Was he okay, was he…? He was sitting on the floor, and one of the soldiers had a gun pointed at him. Beside him, lying curled up, holding his side, was Red—he'd been shot too!

"Take off their masks," one of the soldiers—obviously the officer in charge—ordered.

They ripped the balaclava off Red, and then Jack, and mine was yanked off as well and—

"Jack?" a voice called out. "George? What are you two doing here?"

One of the soldiers obviously recognized us. I turned to the voice. I recognized him too. He looked surprised … no, shocked.

"We can explain!" I said.

"No point in telling us," the officer in charge said. "Jamison and Campbell, you go and get Bill and the Lieutenant-Colonel. Wake them up and get them down here right away. And you don't talk to anybody else or tell anybody what's happened. Just tell them we have a *situation*."

Two of the soldiers hurried away.

"I'm just so glad that you—"

"Not another word," the officer said to me. "Just keep your hands where I can see them." He turned to two of his men. "Put him with the others."

The two soldiers pulled me along and then practically threw me to the ground beside Jack and Red. Three of the soldiers now had their rifles trained on us. That was right. They knew us, but that didn't change the facts. We were still in trouble, big trouble. And what about our mom? My body started to shake and I knew what was going to happen next. I started to cry.

"Stop crying," Jack said out of the corner of his mouth.

"I can't!" I sobbed.

"Stop it. There's nothing to cry about—it's going to be okay."

I didn't believe him. I didn't see any way that this could be okay. I looked past Jack. Red was still holding his side. Blood was dripping from between his fingers and his face was distorted with pain.

"This one is dead," I heard a voice say.

I looked over. There were two soldiers standing over Moose.

"He took four slugs," one of them said. "Two to the chest, one to the neck and one to the leg. Probably dead before he hit the ground."

Before he hit *me*.

There was a commotion at the entrance of the cave. The Lieutenant-Colonel marched in—he was wearing his pants and boots with an untucked nightshirt overtop. Behind him was Bill. His eyes widened and he skidded to a stop as he saw us. And then, behind him, came Little Bill! I couldn't believe that he was here. Why was he here?

His looked at us, but his expression remained steady and calm, as if he had expected this whole scene, including us being part of it.

Little Bill walked forward. "You three," he said, pointing to three of the soldiers, "at the door. Nobody comes, nobody goes. Nobody says a word."

"Yes, sir," one of them said, and then all three soldiers saluted and rushed away.

"I want these two searched, and somebody tend to that man's wounds," he continued.

"Should we call in the doctor?" the Lieutenant-Colonel asked.

"We call nobody until I know more," Little Bill answered. "George, Jack, you come with me."

We got to our feet.

"Bill, you come too."

Little Bill led us down a passage. The ceiling was low and, like the walls, it was cut out of sheer rock. The floor was wet and slippery. He opened a door to reveal an office and he motioned for us to enter. There was a small desk and four chairs and behind that, piled right to the ceiling, were glimmering bars of gold!

"Please sit," Little Bill said. We each took a chair and Little Bill took a seat behind the desk.

Even though it was the middle of the night, Little Bill was dressed in a fresh white shirt, crisp black tie and perfectly creased trousers. We sat down, and Little Bill took a seat behind the desk. Bill didn't sit. He stood right behind us.

"George, are you wounded?" Little Bill asked, pointing to my shirt.

"No, it's not my blood. It belonged to Moose ... to the dead guy."

"Better him than either of you."

"We're fine," Jack said.

Actually, I was hurt. I was banged up in the ribs where Moose had fallen on me, but I didn't think I should mention that right now.

"You had us all pretty worried."

"How did you even know that there was something to worry about?" Jack asked.

"Please, Jack, knowing things is what we do," Little Bill said. "Your mother didn't report for work and you two weren't in school. That was reported to us instantly."

"I sent a man to your house and found it deserted," Bill said.

"And then there was the matter of your family going to stay with your grandmother when we know that both of your grandmothers are deceased."

"How do you know that?" I asked.

"George, remember, we have files on everybody who has ever been associated with the camp."

"So you expected to find us here?" I said.

"This is the last place in the world I expected you to be," Little Bill answered. "Now, tell us what is really happening. Who are those men, and where is your mother?"

"Those men have her!" I blurted out. "Not them, but their boss! You have to help us or they'll kill her! You gotta help her!" I burst into tears again, this time even worse.

Little Bill got up from his seat, circled the desk and came and put a hand on my shoulder.

"It will be all right, George," he said softly.

"It doesn't matter what you do with us," Jack said. "We know what we did was wrong. But we didn't have a choice—we had to bring those men here or they were going to kill our mom. If we have to go to jail we'll go to jail, but you have to save our mother. She didn't do anything wrong ... just us!"

"It's not quite clear to me what you did. Please explain the situation, and try not to leave out any details."

Jack started talking. That was good. I didn't know if I could get any words out. He told them about arriving home and the three men and how they were only after the gold.

"They're not Nazis!" I exclaimed. "They're criminals."

Little Bill nodded. "Organized crime. Do you know their names?"

"Just their first names," Jack said. "The one who's dead, his name is Moose ... but I guess that isn't really his name."

"Probably the name he is known by. And the second man?"

"Red, he's called Red."

"And their boss is Dom," I added. "They mentioned his name."

"Are you getting all of this?" Little Bill asked Bill.

Bill was taking notes. "We'll check our sources. We'll soon know more than their first names."

"Are we going to have to go to jail?" I asked.

"If we have to, we have to," Jack said defiantly. "We didn't have a choice. We had to try to save our mother. We did wrong, and we'll take our punishment like men."

"I understand," Little Bill said. "I don't know if I would have done anything differently for my mother."

"Then we're not in trouble?" I asked.

"I didn't say that," he answered, and my fleeting hopes were dashed. "But on the other hand, I can't help but feel responsible. You see, I was the one who set up this trap."

"What do you mean, 'trap'?" Jack asked.

Little Bill reached back and removed one of the gold bars. He tossed it to Jack, who caught it.

"This isn't gold. This is wood painted to look like gold."

"With the exception of a few real gold bars, that's what they all are. We let it be known, we leaked word, that the gold reserves of England were here on the grounds of Camp X."

"So they're really not here?" I asked.

"Safely where they belong, not here."

"But why would you do that?" I asked. "Why would you pretend that they were here?"

"So that the Nazis wouldn't know where the gold really is, and instead they'd try to break in here to steal it."

"And instead of enemy agents you caught some crooks."

"We already caught a spy ring, two weeks ago, coming in off the lake. Catching organized criminals was not the goal. My only question is how the two of you got involved in this."

"They came to our house. They were waiting there with guns," I said.

"Your house? How would they know anything about you?"

"They said they had an informant inside the camp," Jack explained.

"I don't believe for a second that one of my men could be an informant," Bill said.

"But they knew all about us, and Mr. Krum, and that we knew how to sneak into the camp."

"Are you sure they weren't just bluffing?" Little Bill asked.

"If they were bluffing, how did they know to come and get us in the first place?" Jack asked. "How did they even know that we had sneaked into the camp before?"

Bill didn't answer. His look was one of confusion and concern, as though he was struggling to think through the possibilities.

"I think we have a situation," Little Bill said. "We may have to—"

"What about our mother?" Jack asked, cutting him off.

For one of the first times I could ever remember I saw surprise in Little Bill's face. "Jack, George, I'm so sorry ... of course, getting your mother back is of the utmost concern. We will secure her rescue."

"But we don't even know where she is," I said. "We don't know where they're holding her."

"I'm sure that your friend, Red, will know where your mother is being held, and possibly the name of the leak as well. I will personally arrange for him to provide that information," Little Bill said.

"What if he won't talk?" Jack asked.

"Everybody will talk," Little Bill said. His voice was quiet and calm but there was an ominous quality to what he said.

"How badly is he wounded?" Little Bill asked.

"Shot in the gut. Pretty nasty," Bill told him.

"Come, we have to talk to him, and quickly." Little Bill got up and we all followed him back along the passage to where we'd started.

We found Red there, slumped on the floor, leaning against the wall of the cave. His shirt was off and there was gauze taped to his stomach. The white gauze was stained red with blood. The Lieutenant-Colonel was there, and two of the soldiers kept their rifles trained on him.

Little Bill bent down so he was face to face with Red. Red's eyes were closed and he was as white as a ghost. Was he already dead?

"I need some information," Little Bill said.

Red opened his eyes. "I'm not ... I'm not ... saying anything," he said through gritted teeth.

"You will tell me what I need to know," Little Bill said.

"And if I don't?" he gasped.

"I will wait until you decide to talk. I am in no rush," Little Bill said. "Time is not a factor for me. I am not the one who is bleeding to death."

Red didn't say anything. Would Little Bill really just stand there and let him die?

"With each second, more of your life is dripping away … drop by drop … drop by drop. I have seen so much death over the past years that it hardly has any effect on me. What is another life?"

"Even if I talk it don't matter … I'm dead anyway."

"I assure you, you will not receive a death sentence if you tell us what we need to know," Little Bill said.

"It's not you I'm afraid of," Red said, and then he began to cough violently.

Little Bill waited for the coughing to stop. "If you are referring to your boss, Dom, you have nothing to fear. He will be shot. Besides, do you think he would put his life at risk for you? If he were in your shoes he'd sell you out in a second. You know that."

Red remained silent. He wasn't going to talk.

"Please, Red!" I begged. "We just want to save our mother!"

He looked up at me and then back at Little Bill. "What do you need … need to know?"

I felt a wave of relief wash over me.

"There is an informant in this camp. I need to know the name of that person."

"I don't know the name … I only know that Dom gets information, that he knows lots of stuff … but he never told me who it was. You got to believe me."

"I do," Little Bill said. "Unfortunately, I do. Now, for the more important matter. I need to know where the boys' mother is being held."

Red shook his head. "I don't know for sure ... I don't even know if she's still alive."

"What do you mean?" I demanded. "We had a deal—"

"Please, George, remain silent," Little Bill said. He turned back to Red. "I assume that the plan was to kill her and the boys once you arrived with the gold."

"That was the plan."

"We figured that," Jack said. "We had a plan of our own."

"Where were they holding Mrs. Braun? Where was she when you left?"

"What?" Red asked.

"Where was she being held?"

"With Dom ... Dom had her ... he was ... he was ... at his place."

"At his house. Where is his house?"

"Not his house ... in the city ... down in the city."

"Tell us the address," Little Bill said.

"I ... I don't know the address ... I just know where ... where ..."

"Where is it?" Little Bill asked. There was no answer. He reached over and placed his fingers against the man's neck.

"Is he dead?" Jack asked.

"Not yet, but he will be shortly if we don't get him help, and then he'll be useless to all of us." Little Bill stood up and faced the Lieutenant-Colonel. "Select three of your men, get him into a jeep and drive him to the hospital in Oshawa. They are to say nothing to the guards at the gate as they leave, nothing. You will call and arrange for Dr. McCloud to meet them there. Every person who treats him, every person who even lays eyes on him, will be held in a room until tomorrow morning. No one leaves, no one is allowed to make any phone calls. Is that clear?"

"Perfectly." He selected three men, and two of them picked Red up and carried him away. He groaned slightly as he got to his feet but I didn't think he regained consciousness.

"Now we need to get all available information on this Dom, but as long as we're harbouring an informant we can't use our normal channels here at Camp X. If he finds out we're on to him, then he'll start to tie up loose ends."

"Loose ends like our mother, right?" Jack asked.

"I believe so."

"So you think she's still alive, right?" I asked.

"I'm operating on that assumption, but I'm not going to lie to you," Little Bill said. "It may be too late."

I felt my knees get weak and I thought I was going to collapse to the floor. I put a hand against the wall to steady myself.

"Look, we can find out if she's still alive. We can call and ask to talk to her," Jack said.

"Call? You have a telephone number?" Little Bill asked.

"Yeah, it's the number we called and—"

"You don't understand, boys—as long as we have a number we can find the location!" Bill exclaimed.

"Let me have the number," Little Bill said.

Jack dug into his pocket and pulled out the scrap of paper. It was all folded over and crumpled. He opened it up and—

"Oh, no, it can't be."

"What? What's wrong?" I asked.

Jack turned the paper so I could see it. Where the number had been written there was nothing more than a blur of ink on the water-soaked paper.

CHAPTER FOURTEEN

"IT CAN'T BE," Jack said.

"Let me see the paper," Little Bill said, and he took it from Jack.

"There's nothing ... no numbers ... nothing," Jack said. "It's lost ... our mother is lost."

That brief sense of relief I'd felt was gone, and I now felt more weak and woozy than I had before. I just wanted to sit down—no, curl up in a little ball and cry. That was it, there was no way to find our mother. If she was even still alive, there was no way we could find her now, no way we could rescue her or—

"I need two of your best men in the documents-and-forgeries section—maybe Wilson and Padlowksi—to look at this paper and reclaim the number," Little Bill said.

"Can they do that?" Jack asked.

"I don't think that should present too big a problem. The ink is badly blurred but the greatest concentration should still be at the place of origin, the place where the numbers will be." He turned to the Lieutenant-Colonel. "Have two of your men take this piece of paper, wake up Wilson and Padlowski, and then stand guard. No phone calls, no contact with anybody else."

"I'll have that done," the Lieutenant-Colonel said. He summoned two men over and passed on the piece of paper. The two started off.

"Please, come with me … you and Bill and the boys."

We followed Little Bill back to the office and closed the door as the last of us entered.

"Do you trust Wilson and Padlowski?" Little Bill asked.

"I trust all my men," the Lieutenant-Colonel said.

"In light of what we've just heard, that sense of trust is faulty. That's why I ordered the guard to keep them isolated while they work. Obviously, there is one man who cannot be trusted. As of this moment, I trust only the people in this room. Everyone else is suspect and will not be cleared until we can find the mole."

"The 'mole'?" I asked.

"The informant, the traitor."

"The traitor …" I shook my head slowly. "I don't know why you still trust *us*."

"Boys, there are few men I trust more than the two of you," Little Bill said.

"But after what we did?" I asked, not believing my ears.

"I do not believe," he said, "that you boys would have come here if you had not believed it was the only way to protect your mother. And if you had managed to escape with the gold—and your lives—what then?"

"We were going to turn ourselves in, explain what happened and accept the consequences," Jack said.

"Whatever those consequences were ... or are going to be," I said.

"That is what I suspected you'd say. It's what makes you trustworthy, in my eyes. No matter what these men might have said to you, I believe that you would have done the right thing once your mother was safe, and I can't ask more of you than that."

"We just need to save our mother, that's what matters," Jack said. This time it sounded as though *he* might be thinking about crying.

"As soon as we have the telephone number, and the address that will provide for us, we'll take action. Now, I need you to do one more thing," Little Bill said to the Lieutenant-Colonel. "I want you to wake everyone at the camp and have them gather in the mess hall. I want you to then tell everybody that there has been a successful breach of security. Some unknown enemy agents broke into the camp. It is believed that there were four of them. One was badly wounded and is not expected to live. A second was wounded but made his escape with the two other agents who were not injured. Finally, it is believed that they made off with a large quantity of gold."

"I can do that, but I don't understand the reasons behind it," he said.

"I want the informant to hear that the mission has been successful so that this Dom will be expecting the boys to return with the gold."

"I see. I just wish there were some way for us to figure out who that informant is," Bill said.

"Ah, that is the second part of my plan," Little Bill said. "I need you to select the five men you and the Lieutenant-Colonel suspect could be the informant."

"I don't know if there would be that many."

"It's better to cast the net wider than to miss our quarry completely. This may be our only chance. I'll explain the rest of my plan as I walk you back to head-quarters." He turned to face us. "Boys, you are to remain here. I'll return with the address and we will leave immediately. In the meantime you should try to get some rest. You must be exhausted."

The four of us trudged through the woods, following the creek, back toward the highway. It struck me as incredibly strange that we were with Bill and Little Bill but we still had to try to *escape* from the camp without letting any of the guards see us. Bill had explained that as long as the identity of the informant was still unknown, anyone who saw us might be capable of passing that information to Dom.

We went up the embankment and onto the highway.

"The truck is just over this way," Jack said.

We walked down the centre of the road. It was almost three in the morning and there was no traffic. If we saw anything coming we'd have to scramble into the trees. Jack led us down the little path and we pulled off the branches covering the truck. Bill pulled the keys out of his pocket—he'd taken them from Moose's pocket. He opened the truck and we all climbed in, Bill at the wheel.

Little Bill stood at the door, holding up a hat and coat that belonged to one of the two men. "These might prove very useful," he said. He passed them to me. "Place them in the back."

Bill started the truck. Slowly he backed it up the incline and onto the shoulder of the highway.

"How far do we have to drive?" I asked.

"It will be close to an hour," Little Bill said. "But I don't want to fill you boys with false hope. This is the address listed with the number that you called. It doesn't mean that he's still at that location. And even if he is there, that doesn't mean your mother is."

Or that she's even still alive, I thought but didn't say. There was no need to say what everybody was already thinking. Maybe if I didn't say the words they wouldn't be true.

"How many agents were you able to contact?" Little Bill asked Bill.

"Three."

"I was hoping for more men."

"We may not have quantity, but we have quality. These are three of the very best."

"They may have to be. We have no idea how many men will be at this location. All we can be certain of is that they will be armed and they won't be afraid to shed our blood."

"We'll be ready for whatever they throw at us. Our agents will rendezvous with us in fifty minutes, at a spot approximately two miles from the site."

"Excellent."

"Ideally I would have had three or four more operatives, but some of the men are on assignment, and I had to be sure that everyone I chose was above suspicion," Bill explained.

"That's part of the territory in espionage. It's a dirty game, and the first casualty is trust."

"I was thinking about it, trying to narrow down the list of possible suspects," Little Bill said. "There are a number of factors. Obviously the mole has been at the camp since midsummer. If not, it's unlikely he would have any knowledge of the activities of the boys."

"That makes sense."

"And he had to be there in September, when we

originally planted the idea about the gold," Little Bill added.

"That narrows down the numbers considerably," Bill said.

"And there is one more factor, one important factor. This is somebody who has knowledge of the story of the gold reserves being at the camp but doesn't know that it is simply a story. Somebody who doesn't know it was a trap."

"That all makes perfect sense."

"And of the men who were selected afterwards, the men you and the Lieutenant-Colonel pulled aside and spoke to individually, how many of them would fit the profile?" Little Bill asked.

"Two … no, possibly three … I'd have to look at their personnel files more closely to be certain," Bill said. "But even if it was only one man, that still doesn't mean he's the one who turned traitor."

"You're right. Suspicion is far from proof. Although we may get all the proof we need tonight, if my trap works."

I wanted to ask him more about what he meant but I knew it wasn't my business. Besides, all I really wanted to know was what he had planned to save our mother. I didn't care about any informant, I just cared about getting her out safely.

"When you find the guy, the one that snitched on us, let me have a few minutes alone with him," Jack said bitterly. "He's the guy responsible for all of this happening to us."

That was right. If he hadn't told Dom about us, Dom wouldn't have known to come looking for us, and he wouldn't have kidnapped our mother. Now I wanted him too.

The van slowed down and pulled to the side of the road. Bill turned off the lights. He then flicked them on and off twice. Down the road a pair of headlights answered back. Bill turned the lights on again and pulled back onto the road. He slowed down again and then pulled the van over right beside the car that had answered his signal. The doors opened and three men—all dressed in black—climbed out and approached the passenger side of the van.

"Good evening, gentlemen," Little Bill said.

"Good evening, sir," one of the men replied.

"Climb in and we'll discuss the operation."

The side door opened and the three men climbed in. They looked surprised to see us in the back—I guess that made sense. Nobody would expect a couple of kids to be along on a mission.

"Before we go, I want to make sure everybody understands their role. Especially you, George."

"Me? I have a role?" I asked. I'd thought I was just going to sit in the back of the van.

"You have the most important role. The success of the whole mission rests on your shoulders."

CHAPTER FIFTEEN

THE TRUCK SAT OFF THE ROAD, partially hidden behind a stand of trees. Little Bill was at the wheel, wearing the hat and coat that belonged to Red. Bill and Jack were in the back, and the three agents were surrounding the vehicle, hidden among the trees.

"Do you remember what you're going to say?" Little Bill asked.

"I remember." We'd gone over it three times.

"Good. Now I'm not going to tell you not to be scared, because you should be scared, and they need to see you looking scared if they're to believe you."

"Boy, are *they* going to believe me, because I'm *really* scared."

Little Bill laughed, which caught me by surprise, and I couldn't stop myself—despite everything—from smiling.

"It's ten minutes to four. Everyone should be asleep. Don't be afraid of knocking as loudly as you need to in order to wake them up."

"You're sure that's the house, right?"

"I'm sure that's the house you placed the call to. Whether Dom is there or not we can't guarantee. If he is not there, they'll probably know where he is. You'll have to convince them to either tell you or take you there. Understand?"

"I understand. I'll convince them."

"Good. I'm counting on you."

"Mom's counting on you," Jack said from the back.

"I know." I was all too aware of that fact.

"Maybe it would be better if I went," Jack said.

"No, it's better that they think you're here with the truck, watching Red, maybe ready to make a getaway," Little Bill explained. "It has to be George."

"I can do it," I said. "I know I can." I wasn't sure if I was trying to convince Jack, Little Bill or myself.

"George," Little Bill said, "you know I would never want to place you in danger unnecessarily, but this is the best chance we have of rescuing your mother. I have complete faith in you, George," he said. "I know you can do this."

"Me too," Jack said.

"You do?" I asked in surprise.

"Yeah. I just would rather it was me so you wouldn't have to go up there by yourself, that's all."

"Thanks," I said.

"Better get going. And don't forget to tell him how many bars of gold were stolen. You remember the number, right?"

"Twenty-one."

"Exactly. And I need you to remember exactly what he says, if anything, when you tell him that number."

"I'll remember," I said, although I didn't understand why that was so important.

I climbed out of the truck and closed the door as silently as I could. I moved up onto the road and then started down the deserted street. I stopped at the bottom of the driveway and looked up at the house. The lights were all off. The house was dark, just like every other house on the street. Everybody was asleep. Silently I walked up the driveway. There were three cars parked by the garage. One of them looked like the car the men had taken our mother away in just the night before. Could that be possible? It seemed like a week ago ... a lifetime ago.

I stopped at the front door. I took a couple of deep breaths and thought things through one more time, thought about what I was going to say. Then I reached up and pounded my fist against the door. I was startled by the power of my blows—they sounded more like cannon fire than knocking. I pounded again.

I saw a light come on through the window. Somebody was up, but with all the sound I'd made I could have woken the dead ... *The dead*. No, I couldn't let my mind go there.

The door opened and a large man was standing there. He wore a fierce expression and I felt a rush of fear.

I took a deep breath. "I need to see Dom."

"Do you? And what makes you think we know anybody named Dom?" he growled.

"I know you do, and unless you want him to lose a fortune in gold you'd better get him or—"

Dom appeared beside the man. He opened the door wider, grabbed me by the arm and yanked me inside!

"Where's my gold?" he demanded.

"It's in the truck, with Red!"

He started out the door, then stopped and turned around. "I don't see a truck! Where's my gold?"

"Before I tell you where you can get the gold, we have to make a deal."

He reached out, grabbed me by my shirt collar and lifted me off my feet, pulling me up into his face, staring at me, eye to eye, his breath foul.

"You want a deal? I'll give you a deal. You tell me where my gold is and I won't kill you right now!"

"You kill me and you'll never get your gold. Is my life worth that much to you?" I asked, saying the lines that I'd been told to say and that I'd rehearsed.

His lip curled into a smile—really more a smirk. He let me down.

"I have something for you," I said, and I started to reach into the cloth bag I was carrying, the bag Little Bill had given me.

Instantly there were three guns pointed at me.

"No, no, I don't have a weapon," I gasped as I put my hands up. "I have something for you. Can I get it?" It wasn't a weapon. It was more like a shield I could hide behind.

"Slowly," Dom said.

I opened the bag and pulled out a bar of gold. It was real, hard and smooth and heavy in my hands.

I could see Dom's eyes widen. He reached out and took it from me.

"Beautiful," Dom said as he held it up.

It *was* beautiful.

"The other twenty bars are in the truck," I said.

"Twenty? Don't you mean twenty-two?" he asked.

"I guess so … I really don't know … they're all in the truck."

"There'd better be twenty-two more bars. You got away with twenty-three bars, I know that, so don't try and cheat me!"

That was the response I was supposed to remember. Dom thought that twenty-*three,* not twenty-*one,* bars were stolen.

"Nobody is trying to cheat you. Everything we took is yours. You can ask Red. He's wounded pretty bad, but he's there. Moose was shot and we couldn't get him out. I don't know if he's okay or if … if … if he's …"

"He's in the hospital," Dom said.

"How do you know that?"

"I know lots of things. Now, all I need to know is what you want before you take me to my gold."

"I need to know my mother is okay."

"She's okay."

"I want to see her."

"Isn't my word good enough for you?" he asked.

I shook my head. "Until I see her you don't see the gold."

"How'd you find me, anyway?" he asked. "How'd you get here?"

"What?"

"How'd you get here? Did you walk?"

"Part of the way, after I was dropped off."

"You telling me that Red is part of this scheme?" he demanded.

"I'm telling you that Red isn't in any shape to be part of anything. He's hurt, wounded, and if you don't do something fast he's probably going to *die*."

He shrugged. "Not my concern. What's to stop me from just putting a bullet in your head, sending out my men, searching the neighbourhood and finding that truck?"

"There's nothing to stop you from shooting me, I guess, but if Jack doesn't see me walk out of here in the next couple of minutes, then he'll run back to that truck, get in, drive away and the only gold you see will be on the badges of the cops he goes to get."

"I don't think he'd do that."

"You're wrong. Maybe you don't care about Moose or Red or any of these guys," I said, gesturing to the men standing around us, "but we're *really* family. If I don't come back he'll know Mom and I are dead, and he'll make sure you pay for it."

"You bluffing me, kid?"

"You want to risk finding out?" I asked back.

He laughed, and that caught me off guard. He looked over his shoulder. "Go and get the kids' mother." Two men disappeared down a corridor.

"You got guts, kid," he said.

And my plan is to keep them inside of me, I thought, but I kept my mouth closed.

I heard the sound of somebody coming down the hall and I looked up. It was Mom! I started to rush toward her when Dom held out a hand and stopped me.

"George! You're hurt!" she screamed out, a look of terror on her face.

"No," I said, shaking my head, "I'm fine." Then I realized why she thought that. The blood—Moose's blood—had left a large red stain on the front of my shirt.

"It's not mine. It's from one of the mobsters. Are you okay?"

"Doesn't she look fine?" Dom answered for her. "Now that you see she's alive, you need to keep your end of the bargain. You need to bring the gold here."

"I was thinking I'd bring *you* to *it*," I said.

"Nope, it isn't going to happen that way. I stay here, with your mother, and you bring the gold to me."

That wasn't how we had it planned. I was supposed to bring him and his men out of the house and then, once they were in the open, they could be easily captured. I had to think fast.

"I'm going to need some help," I said. "Moose is gone and Red can't even carry himself. I need some of your men to come and carry the gold—it's heavy."

He was still holding the gold bar in his hand. "I can see that." He turned to face his men. "You, you and you, go with the kid."

I turned to start out the door but he grabbed me by the arm. "And remember, no tricks. Your mother's still in here with me."

"No tricks from us," I said. "And just so you know, we're ready for any tricks you might have planned … like killing us all after you get the gold."

"Come on, kid, I wouldn't do that. You have my word."

"Your word isn't good enough. Before we drove here we got Red to tell us everything, including your name. We stopped, wrote a letter and mailed it to one of our relatives."

"You did *what*?" he exclaimed.

"The letter is addressed to us. If we walk out of here we go and get the letter and rip it up. If we don't walk out, if nobody ever sees us again, then she'll open that letter and turn it over to the authorities."

"You're bluffing."

"Not bluffing. Just taking care of things."

"Even if we did kill all of you, do you really think that letter would mean anything? Even with that letter there still isn't proof I was involved. The police won't be able to do anything to us. No court can convict us without proof," he snorted.

"It isn't the police you should be worried about. Those guys at Camp X, they don't need proof and they don't need a court. They'll just come and kill you. Here, there, wherever you go. You'll be a rich guy waiting to be a *dead* rich guy. I know because I know them. You kill us now, you're just killing yourself later."

He wasn't laughing. He wasn't smiling. He was believing what I was saying.

CHAPTER SIXTEEN

I WALKED SLOWLY, deliberately, making sure that my feet dragged enough to warn of our arrival. My whole body was shaking, and it had nothing to do with the damp night air. Two of Dom's men flanked me and a third was a few steps behind. I kept looking back over my shoulder, past him, to see if anybody else was coming. I didn't want anything, or anybody, to be a surprise.

"How far we gotta walk?" the man on my left asked.

"Not far."

"You figure they're still there?" the man on the other side asked.

"Of course."

"You sure? I'm guessing *my* brother would sell *me* out for a fortune in gold," one of the mobsters said.

The other two laughed.

"Maybe your brother, but not mine. We weren't raised that way," I said, and again the other two laughed—this time at me.

"Funny, kid. We'll see if you're still laughing at the end of the night."

That was a threat, plain and simple. I knew that they were all armed and dangerous. I would have been a lot more scared if it hadn't been for the fact that I knew I had a few guys with guns on my side.

We kept walking. I was beginning to worry. It seemed to me I hadn't walked that far to get to the house. I thought the truck should have been closer. They wouldn't have moved it … would they? For a split second I had the irrational fear that Jack *had* taken off with the gold, before I remembered that there really wasn't any gold, and Bill and Little Bill were with him, and finally, Jack just wouldn't do that.

"There's the truck," I said, pointing ahead, relieved that I'd found it.

"I don't see nothing," one of the men said.

"It's there, just off to the side of the road."

Really, I could only make out a vague outline. It was so dark and so well hidden in the shadows that if I hadn't known it was there we would have walked right past it.

I looked to my left. The mobster had pulled out his gun. So had the guy to my right. I didn't need to look back to know the third was doing the same.

"You think Red is going to shoot one of you?" I asked.

"No sense in taking any chances."

"How about if we take no chances," I said. "You three just stay behind and let me tip them off that it's you. That way, if Red takes a shot at anybody it'll be me."

The one gunman shrugged. "Sure, kid, your funeral."

They hung back while I walked toward the van. "It's me, George!" I yelled out. "There's nothing to worry about." I kept walking. "I've brought help … *three* people … three of Dom's men … but not Dom, he stayed at the house."

I wanted them to know the numbers but also to know that Dom was really at the house—back at the house with our mother. That meant that nobody would be firing any shots. We were close enough to the house that they'd be able to hear gunfire, and then there was no telling what might happen.

I walked over to the driver's side window. Somebody was in the driver's seat, his head down almost on the steering wheel and his arms up to hide his face. Red's hat was on his head, and along with his coat it made for a perfect disguise. Jack sat in the passenger seat.

"Tell them that Red is almost dead," Jack said quietly to me.

"Come quick," I shouted back to the men. "Red is hardly breathing. He's almost dead."

Two of the men rushed toward the passenger side, while the other pushed me out of the way and leaned in the driver's window.

"Red, are you—?"

It was Little Bill under the hat, and he sat up and aimed his pistol square at the man's face. At the same instant Bill burst out of the side door, and the three agents appeared out of nowhere and took the other two men prisoner. All three stood there, hands up, shocked looks on their faces. Somehow the whole scene struck me as funny. I had to stop myself from laughing out loud.

"All three of you, put your hands on top of your heads," Bill said.

They did as they were ordered.

"Now I have a few questions," Little Bill began.

"We're not talking," one of them snarled.

"And do you speak for the group?" Little Bill asked.

"We don't talk to nobody."

"Fine, then I won't waste time asking you anything further." Little Bill reached into an inside pocket of his jacket and pulled out a small, dark piece of metal. He started to screw it onto the barrel of his pistol.

"This is a silencer," he said, his voice quiet and calm. "Its purpose is to make a gunshot so muffled that it can't be heard more than a few feet away. So, for example, if I were to shoot this gun right here they most certainly wouldn't hear it back at the house."

He took the gun and pushed it into the face of the man who had said they weren't going to talk.

"Since you will not talk, you are of no value to me except as an example to the other two of what happens to somebody who doesn't cooperate. I'm going to kill you."

"You can't do that!" he said, his voice quavering.

"Of course I can. I can do whatever I want. I am not required to arrest you or follow any of the laws of this land. I am above the laws of this country. I am fully authorized to simply kill anybody who represents a threat to our country. You, sir, are a threat, so I will shoot you."

He then looked at the second man. "And after I have shot him I will ask you to talk. And if you refuse I will shoot you in a similar manner and then ask the third man," he said, pointing at the last thug. "And if all three of you refuse to talk you will certainly have gained my utmost respect for being men of honour who would give up your lives rather than give up information. I will salute you, but you will most certainly, nevertheless, be dead."

His voice was so calm, so matter-of-fact, I had no doubt that what he was saying was the truth. He would kill them.

"Jack, George, perhaps it is best that you go to the other side of the truck for this."

I started to walk away but Jack grabbed my arm.

"We're not going anywhere," he said.

I wanted to go but I had no choice now.

"These guys are part of the gang that kidnapped our mother. I want to see them get what they deserve."

Jack sounded so convincing that I didn't know if he was just playing along or if he was serious.

"As you wish," Little Bill said. He turned back to face the first man. "Now that you fully understand my position, I want to give you the opportunity to change your mind. Are you willing to answer my questions?"

"I'll answer!" he blurted out. "What do you want to know?"

"Excellent." He removed the gun from the man's face. "I need to know how many more of Dom's men are in the house."

"Five, he has five men," he said.

"Are you lying?" Little Bill asked.

"No, that's the God's honest truth! Honest!"

"So including Dom, there are six men. And do they simply have sidearms or do they have access to other weapons, such as rifles or shotguns?"

"He's got everything in the house," he said. "Twelve-gauge shotguns, some Enfield rifles."

"He even has some hand grenades," the second man volunteered.

"And some dynamite," the third added.

It seemed like everybody was willing to talk now.

"Quite the arsenal," Little Bill said. "I guess we should be grateful that he doesn't have a bazooka. He doesn't have a bazooka in there, does he?"

"Um … no," the man answered.

"That was my attempt at a little levity, a little humour. Next question: how many exits are there?"

"Three, I guess," the first man said.

"No, four," the second corrected him.

The first shook his head. "You're wrong, there are only three. Front and back doors, and a door at the far side."

"No, *you're* wrong. There's also the coal chute in the basement."

"That ain't a door."

"You can get in or out through there. It's an exit!"

"I think four is the correct answer," Little Bill said. "Now, finally, where are they holding Mrs. Braun?"

"She's been locked in a room up on the second floor, but she was right there in the room off the entrance when we left."

"I see. Thank you for your cooperation. This is a much better outcome than the alternatives. Now I need all three of you to take off your clothes."

"What?"

"Your clothing, take it off. We require it. Strip down to your underpants."

"You gotta be joking."

"No joke." Little Bill reached out, took hold of the fabric of the one man's topcoat and rubbed it between his fingers. "Very nice, certainly nicer than anything I could ever afford. Obviously crime *does* pay. Now, remove your clothing, and please, if I have to repeat my request I will not be *nearly* so polite."

CHAPTER SEVENTEEN

THE THREE GANGSTERS were lying on the ground.
They were in their undershirts and shorts and were
tied up, ropes around their ankles, wrists and necks.
There was a rag—actually one of their own socks—
stuffed in each of their mouths and held in place with
tape. Just off to the side Bill and two of the agents
were arguing over which clothes from which of the
gangsters fit them best.

"George, before we go in I need to ask you a question. Did you tell this Dom fellow how many bars of
gold you had in the truck?"

"I told him that there were twenty bars in the truck
plus the one I gave him, for a total of twenty-one—
just what you told me to say."

"And what did he say when you told him that?"

"He told me that I didn't have twenty-*one* bars, I
had twenty-*three*."

"Are you sure that was the number he said?
Positive?"

"I'm positive. You told me it was important to
remember, so I know that's what he said."

"You did very well, George," Little Bill said.

"Thanks. I just did what I had to do."

"No, you did more than that. You modified the plan when the situation changed, as a good operative should. Now, you still have one more task. Are you ready? Are you both ready?" He looked at Jack as well.

"We're ready," we agreed.

"I must also warn you that this operation will be extremely dangerous. You are entering an unpredictable, potentially lethal situation. It is highly likely that somebody will die—perhaps many people will die—before this is resolved."

"We'll take our chances. We just want to make sure our mom is safe," Jack said.

Little Bill didn't answer at first. "I cannot guarantee her safety, or the safety of either of you boys. Now I need to be sure: do you still wish to be part of the plan?"

"I don't see how you could do it without us," Jack said.

"We could have you remain here at the truck and watch the prisoners. Then we could rush the building, perhaps go in through the coal chute. There are alternatives."

"Nothing as good as this plan," I said. "This is the best chance of getting our mom out alive, so we need to do this."

"I agree, and I appreciate your courage. Again, I want you both to know that you are not just helping to save your mother, you are also serving your country."

"We're just trying to get our mother out," Jack said.

"And trying to make up for what we did," I added.

Bill reappeared. "What do you think of my new clothes?" he asked.

"Very becoming. Perhaps after the war is over you could find employment as one of those models in the Eaton's catalogue selling men's clothing."

All three of us laughed.

"Twenty-three," Little Bill told Bill.

"Twenty-three?"

Little Bill nodded.

"I'm not completely surprised," Bill said. "I'll take care of the problem as soon as we get back."

"Perhaps not immediately."

"But wouldn't it be better to deal with it before he can do any more damage?"

"We need to assess the situation. First we need to know if he is leaking information to anybody else."

"Give me twenty minutes alone with him and we'll know everything we need to know," Bill said.

"I have no doubt you could get that information, but we might lose as much as we gain."

"How could that be?" Bill asked.

"Because then you won't be able to use him any more," I blurted out.

"Very good," Little Bill said. "Bravo, George, you truly have the makings of a first-class operative."

I felt my chest swell with pride.

"Somebody want to explain it to me?" Jack said.

"Certainly. Knowing about the informant—but with him not knowing we know—we can feed the man information we want him to pass on, to mislead others. It might be better for us to allow him to stay in place—at least for now."

Little Bill walked over to the stand of trees where the three gangsters were tied up.

"Gentlemen, I need you to fully appreciate the way that you are bound. There are the obvious ropes around your wrists and ankles, but I want you to pay particular attention to the loop that is around your neck."

I hadn't really noticed that until he mentioned it. Just under their chins there was a loop of rope that led down to their ankles.

"The loop is fairly snug at this point, but if you move your feet or hands the struggling will cause the rope to tighten. In fact, if you struggle too much you might actually cut off your air supply *completely*. You might just lose consciousness due to air loss. You might even strangle yourself to death. It would be a most uncomfortable way to die, so please, for your own sakes, move as little as possible and do not attempt to escape. Oh, and try very hard not to sneeze."

Little Bill walked away and we followed him.

"Everybody please gather around," he said, and all six of us crowded around him.

"We all know our roles. We know what we must do. We are placing our lives in each other's hands. I want to assure you that I have complete faith and confidence in each and every member of this team. I *know* we will succeed."

Jack drove the truck slowly up to the end of the driveway, lights off, and then pulled it to a stop. He turned off the engine and put on the emergency brake.

"Okay, we're here," he said.

"Jack, George, if bullets start flying you two are to hit the floor and stay there until I tell you it's safe to get up," Little Bill said.

"We'll stay down," I said.

"I'd feel better if I had a gun," Jack said.

"Strange, I think I'd feel rather worse," Little Bill said, and Bill and the two agents in the truck laughed. "No guns for the boys. And everybody else, remember, if we can, we want to take the leader, Dom, alive. Shoot him if you must, but do try your best to avoid killing him. Let's go."

Jack and I got out of the truck first. Next, Bill, dressed like one of the gangsters, climbed out the side door. Next came Little Bill—he was still playing the wounded Red—and then two more agents, all of them dressed in the fancy clothing and fedora hats of the men lying in their underwear in the woods. All of them had their hats pulled down so that the brims cast shadows over their faces, making it impossible to make out who they were.

We'd dropped the final agent off at the end of the street. He was circling the house, hoping to come through the back once we'd got everybody's attention focused on the front of the house.

Little Bill flung an arm around Bill and one of the other agents. They had to look as though they were carrying the "wounded" man into the house.

"Slow and easy," Little Bill said softly.

Jack and I led the way up the driveway. We had to be first to partially block the view of those watching from inside the house, but to also avert suspicion. If we were there, a couple of kids, then everything had to be pretty innocent, going the way they wanted it all to go.

I looked up. There were faces at the living-room window, and I could also make out the image of two thugs standing at the door, waiting for us.

We reached the top of the porch stairs and one of the gangsters opened the door for us. I walked in and looked around. Neither Dom nor my mother was anywhere to be seen.

"Aren't you going to help Red?" Jack asked the two thugs.

"Sure, of course."

They practically tripped over each other as they squeezed through the door and stumbled down the steps. And then, like lightning, Bill and the agent on the other side of Little Bill reached up and smashed the men on the heads! The two of them dropped like rocks to the ground! Little Bill burst through the door, almost immediately followed by the other three. The two agents ran into the living room.

"Hands up!" one of them said.

I couldn't see around the corner but the silence spoke volumes. I could picture those men who had been staring out the window frozen in place with their hands in the air.

Little Bill pointed to the room off to the other side and Bill moved through the door. Little Bill continued straight down the hall, his gun leading the way, held in both hands, waist high.

"George," Jack whispered. "You follow Bill and I'll go with Little Bill."

I grabbed his arm as he started away. "Are you crazy?" I hissed at him. "We gotta stay here."

"We gotta find Mom," he said.

He shrugged off my arm and started down the darkened hallway. I couldn't even see Little Bill. This was crazy! We were far better to just stay put. If we went any farther we could just get in the way ... maybe even get in the way of a bullet. I knew staying was the smart thing to do. I also knew I wasn't going to be doing the smart thing.

I doubled back and ducked into the room where Bill had disappeared. It was dark, the only light coming in from the hall. Standing in the only lit spot didn't seem like the right thing to do. I dropped to the floor and on all fours began moving forward. Quickly my eyes adjusted. It was dim, but not dark.

I could make out the furniture—a chair and a big sofa, and there was a piano. I worked my way around the room, staying close to the wall, until I came to another doorway. Off to the left was another hall, probably doubling back to where Jack had gone. To the right was a set of stairs leading to the second floor. That was where they'd been holding my mother. Since she wasn't in the living room, where I'd last seen her, they must have taken her back upstairs.

Slowly, I crawled over to the stairs. Like a little dog I started to climb up, step by step. There was a runner in the centre and I stayed right in the middle of that, the better to silence whatever sounds I might be making. There was a little bit of light coming down the stairs and I followed it upward. I stopped at the top, peeking around the banister, using it as a shield. I could see five—no, six doors. One of the doors—the one closest—was slightly open. The next door was closed but there was light coming out from under the edge. That was the room I needed to get to. I started crawling forward. Low to the ground seemed like the best place to be.

Suddenly the air exploded with gunfire. I practically jumped before I scrambled forward and then rolled through the open door. I pulled it almost completely closed to shield myself. There were five shots, no six, or seven, or ten—so many that I couldn't even count them! They sounded like they were coming from downstairs. Then there was silence. What had happened? I stayed perfectly still, trying to think through my options. Who had shot whom? Was everybody okay?

"I want to know what's happening out there!" yelled out a voice. It was Dom's, and it sounded close. "Somebody talk to me!"

There was silence.

"John … Simon … Nick!" Dom yelled. "Somebody talk to me, tell me what's happening!"

Again there was no answer.

"They aren't able to talk to you." It was Little Bill. His voice—as always—was calm and in control. "Four of your men are dead and the rest are being held at gunpoint."

"Who are you?" Dom called back. He sounded nearly as calm as Little Bill.

"I am the man who will help decide whether you will walk out of this situation or be carried out of it, feet first."

"You'd better know that if you kill me I won't be the only one to die. I have a hostage."

A hostage. That could only mean …

"And you really wouldn't want this nice lady to get shot, would you?" Dom asked.

There was no answer right away.

"I would prefer that nobody get killed, but that decision will be up to you. I'd rather make a deal that could benefit us all."

"Why would you make a deal with me?" Dom asked.

"Because you have something we want. We want the name of your contact inside the camp."

"What if I told you I didn't know what you were talking about?" Dom asked.

"Then I'd tell you that you were lying. Would you like to make a deal?"

"I would. Here's my deal. I walk out of here with this lady and nobody follows me, and then I let her go a few miles from here. How's that sound for a deal? I'm coming out now and I'm going to make my way to the stairs. Anybody tries to stop me … if I even see anybody … I'm going to shoot her."

"Wait!" Little Bill yelled out. "First let me clear the house so that nothing happens accidentally." There was a slight pause. "I want all agents to leave the premises immediately … go off the property, and leave the keys in the truck!"

He couldn't be serious about that! How could he trust this man to keep up his end of the bargain? He could get away and then just keep our mother prisoner, or even shoot her and dump her on the side of the road.

"The house is clear," Little Bill called out.

"I'm coming out!" Dom yelled. "And don't try anything or she's dead!"

The door opened and light spilled into the hall. Mom emerged from the room. Dom was right behind her, one arm around her neck holding her close, his other hand holding a gun to her head.

"I'm coming out too." It was Little Bill. He stepped out of the shadows at the far end of the hall. "I do not have a weapon," he said. His hands were up in the air.

"You the guy running this operation?" Dom asked.

Little Bill nodded.

"I should just shoot you."

"You might as well just shoot yourself too. How about if you leave the woman and take me instead? I'm a far more valuable hostage than she is. She's just somebody's mother, a secretary. Let me go with you."

"I don't know *who* you are, but I sure know *what* you are," Dom said. "You're one of those spies—you know how to kill people. You just stay right where you are and don't come any closer."

"As you wish," Little Bill said.

Dom was probably smart not to let Little Bill get closer. He started backing away from where Little Bill was standing, my mother between them as a shield, being dragged along. They were backing up toward me. I had the urge to sink deeper into the shadows but that wouldn't help her. I had to do something. In just a few seconds he'd be right outside the doorway where I was hidden, and in a few seconds after that he'd be past and gone. He kept backing up. He was there, just opposite the door, but what could I do? What would Jack do? Instantly I knew.

I flung myself against the door with all my weight and power. The door flew out and smashed against the side of his head with a sickening crash. He crumpled to the ground and his gun hit the floor and then bounced down the stairs!

I stood there, stunned, staring down at Dom. I looked up at my mother. She looked as stunned as I felt.

Out of nowhere Bill materialized, and then one of the agents and Little Bill, and they were all standing around us.

"George!" my mother yelled, and she wrapped her arms around me. She started to cry.

"It's all over," I said as I held on to her. "It's all over now."

CHAPTER EIGHTEEN

DOM WAS CARRIED OUT of the house. He was still unconscious, but he was alive.

"What's going to happen to him now?" Jack asked.

"He'll be interrogated," Little Bill told us. "We're going to get the information we need from him confirming the identity of the informant."

"Confirming?" I asked.

"Yes. We know who it is. Dom's response that I asked you to remember when you said there were twenty-one bars of gold?"

"Yeah—he said there were twenty-three."

"We decided on five people who might be the informant," Bill explained. "Little Bill had us tell each of them, privately, that some gold bars had been stolen, only we told each of them a different number. The man who was told that twenty-three were stolen was obviously the man who contacted Dom. That man is the informant."

"That was great thinking," I said.

"And after Dom is interrogated he will be put someplace where he will never bother anybody again for the rest of his life," Little Bill said.

"Were you really going to let him walk out of here with our mother?" I asked.

Little Bill shook his head. "He was going to be shot, one bullet to the head, instant death, so instant that he couldn't have pulled the trigger."

"I guess I should have just let things happen," I said.

"Better than letting things happen is making things happen. What you did was right." He turned to my mother. "You must be exhausted."

"I think I could sleep for a week," she said.

"Come, sit." Little Bill offered her a comfortable armchair and she practically collapsed into it. She looked as limp as a rag doll. Jack and I sat down on chairs beside hers.

"You will have sufficient time to recover. You won't be returning to work for at least three or four days," Little Bill said.

"I'm sure I'll be fine by tomorrow," our mother said. "I really should get back to work."

"That isn't possible. As far as the people at Camp 30 know, you have the measles and you are staying with your mother, so we have to stick with that story. If you return too soon there will be too many questions."

"Does that mean we don't go to school either?"

"You do not. In fact, you will not even be going home for the next three days."

"Where will we stay?" I asked.

"You will be staying at one of our safe houses for a while. That will allow your cover story to remain intact. As well, we have to debrief you."

"What does that mean?" our mother asked.

"We have to ask you questions about everything that happened," Bill explained. "Standard practice. And of course, you realize that, other than talking to us, you will not be allowed to tell anybody about anything that happened."

"I hardly *know* what happened," Mom said.

Little Bill turned to her with a sympathetic look. "Of course. You must have a thousand questions."

"A thousand? More like a million. I don't even know what to ask or where to begin," she said.

"That is most understandable. This has certainly been an unbelievable series of events."

"I just can't imagine that my boys have been involved in any of this."

"I think that's why it is so hard for you. You're their mother and you see them as your boys. I don't see them that way." He paused. "I see them as two remarkable young men ... men who are as capable and resourceful and brave as almost any men I have ever known. You should be very proud of them."

"I am proud ... I've always been proud ... I just don't understand. Those things that that mobster said, about the boys being involved in events at Camp X ... at least some of it must be true."

"I am not sure what exactly he told you, but they were indeed involved in many important activities."

She turned to face Jack and me. "How did this all happen?"

"Um ... um ... I don't think we can't talk about it," I said.

"You can't tell your own mother?"

"We can't tell *anybody*," Jack explained. "If we did, we'd get in big—"

"Boys, I think in this case the Official Secrets Act is overruled by the Official Mothers Act. You can tell her what she needs to know."

"We can?"

Little Bill nodded.

"Everything?" I asked.

"Everything," Little Bill said.

"Yes, I want to hear *everything*."

I looked at Jack, and he looked at me and then down at the floor. Funny, he was always telling me to shut up and he'd do the talking. He didn't look like he wanted to do the talking now. I knew what he was thinking, though, because I was thinking the same thing. After all that we'd gone through, all the ways we'd been threatened and almost killed, after everything that had happened, telling Mom was going to be harder than any of it.

I took a deep breath. "Mom ... honestly ... we were really just minding our own business when ..."

AUTHOR'S NOTE

MY THANKS, AGAIN, to Lynn Philip Hodgson, the world expert on Camp X, for all his assistance in researching this novel. For further information about the real Camp X, including a full photo gallery and teacher and student resource, go to his website at **www.camp-x.com**.

Never doubt that a small group of thoughtful committed citizens can change the world. Indeed, it is the only thing that ever has.

— MARGARET MEAD

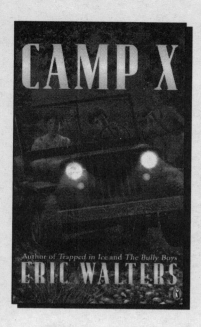

CAMP X

FIND OUT HOW THE ADVENTURE BEGINS!

Every kid dreams of being a secret agent who must sneak behind enemy lines to retrieve valuable information. But what if you discovered a secret military base in your own town? And you couldn't tell anyone about it, not even your mother?

Camp X is the first book in Eric Walters's fast-paced series about Canada's legendary military spy camp!

 penguin.ca   www.ericwalters.net

In this action-packed sequel to *Camp X*, Jack and George have barely recovered from their ordeal when their lives are disrupted once again. Informed that they may still be in danger, they are relocated to Bowmanville, where their mother has been offered a clerking job in a prison of war camp holding the highest ranking German officers.

"With some moments of prickly fear, this is a spirited read."—*The Standard* (St. Catharines, ON)